FITZ RECEIVES A
FEW CALLING CARDS

I walked out of the city room and down to my clunker on East 40th Street, relieved in a way that it was all over. The damned door wouldn't open again. I had to bend over to try to yank it open, and suddenly a window in the parking garage behind me blew apart as though smashed by a baseball bat.

I half straightened up and turned around to look. And then the window next to the first one blew apart. I heard it that time: *Bang!* A sharp, quick report, like a firecracker. A bolt of lightning went through my chest, a terrifying jab of fright, and I was down on the sidewalk beside my car. A squeal of tires, and a million years later I looked up. A third shot had put a dent in the door on the driver's side.

ORDINARY MURDER

"The style is breezy, the clues play fair, and ... the settings are the real McCoy."

— The *Daily News*

MURDER ON THE HUDSON

"The smart dialogue and breezy writing are as New Yorkish as the subways and Times Square....He also knows the ins and outs of the city room, and he sprinkles his book with a few pleasant digressions about fourth-estate eccentrics."

— *The New York Times Book Review*

Also by Don Flynn

MURDER ISN'T ENOUGH
MURDER ON THE HUDSON
ORDINARY MURDER

MURDER IN A-FLAT
DON FLYNN

JOVE BOOKS, NEW YORK

This Jove book contains the complete
text of the original hardcover edition.
It was printed from new film.

MURDER IN A-FLAT

A Jove Book / published by arrangement with
Walker and Company

PRINTING HISTORY
Jove edition / July 1990

All rights reserved.
Copyright © 1988 by Donald R. Flynn and Charlotte J. Flynn.
This book may not be reproduced in whole or in part,
by mimeograph or any other means, without permission.
For information address: Walker and Company,
720 Fifth Avenue, New York, New York 10019.

ISBN: 0-515-10349-7

Jove Books are published by The Berkley Publishing Group,
200 Madison Avenue, New York, New York 10016.
The name "JOVE" and the "J" logo
are trademarks belonging to Jove Publications, Inc.

PRINTED IN THE UNITED STATES OF AMERICA

10 9 8 7 6 5 4 3 2 1

For Al and Laila...
  harmoniously

MURDER IN A-FLAT

1

"CONSIDER THAT EVERYTHING is opinion," advises Marcus Aurelius. The precepts of the ancient Roman emperor occurred to me when Erik Halvorsen, fiddler, played his final note. For it was opinion that set a higher value on a fiddle than on the fiddler.

Hally, as he was called, was the kind of guy you might sometimes notice hurrying through the Times Square theater district, a dark French beret pulled down over the top of his balding head, carrying his fiddle case, his wide eyes alert, leaning slightly forward as he strode along. For Hally was always in a hurry. He was usually playing as a fiddler in the pit of a Broadway musical, but in his heart, as in the heart of all pit fiddlers, Hally was a violinist.

I don't want you to think that this was an idle dream. Because Erik Halvorsen played at Carnegie Hall, too, and at Lincoln Center, and he also played recording dates for television commercials and movie soundtracks. That's the way it is for a fiddle player in New York City—for almost all musicians, in fact—if they're making a living. The only classical musicians with any kind of security are those with chairs in the New York Philharmonic or at the Metropolitan Opera. Others have to hustle, sometimes subbing at the Philharmonic or at the Met, and always dream of doing a solo standing up in front of the orchestra at Avery Fisher Hall at Lincoln Center. But most working musicians know that they must also play for perfume jingles and hold on to that job in the pit of "The Phantom of the Opera." It isn't easy to make a living as a musician in the Big Apple, as, indeed, it isn't easy to make a living at anything.

I met Hally in the usual way, by following a pretty girl on the street. Well, not exactly following her. This elegant slim creature with the bluest of eyes and the goldest of hair came gliding into the *New York Daily Press* one day with a press release about a concert series she was doing.

I first saw her walking along ahead of me on East 42nd Street and found myself more or less mesmerized by her lovely being. I experienced that probably wishful sensation that we were walking together, that, in fact, we knew each other, and that when I caught up with her we would begin chatting away like close friends. But, of course, I didn't know her, and kept behind her. But then she walked into the Daily Press building, and so did I. And she walked onto the elevator, and so did I. And there we were face-to-face, and my foolish, longing head went into a swoon.

"Excuse me," she said then, and my swoon slid into confusion. Was this ethereal, blonde vision speaking to me, a lowly inkstained wretch?

A look at her inquiring face. She was.

"Yes?"

"Are you a reporter?"

I'm afraid I blushed at that, and admitted I was.

"I sort of thought so," she smiled winsomely. "You look like one."

I wasn't sure I knew what that meant, although it's true that reporters do have a certain look about them, which is not necessarily the image of anybody in a *New Yorker* magazine men's fashion ad.

"You look like someone, too," I blurted out. "A model." Trying in my elfin way to lay on the charm.

"A what!" The blue eyes narrowed, and the waterfall hair bounced. She was annoyed.

"Well ... I mean ..."

"A *model*? Do I look that . . . *shallow* to you?"

No, no, I thought anxiously. Deep, very deep. And thoroughly delicious. But it was too late. My obvious oafishness had hit a flat note, and the elegant beauty wasn't smiling anymore. Now, she was suddenly all business.

"Could you tell me whom I should see about getting an item in the paper?" she asked.

"What kind of item?"

"Probably not one that somebody like you would handle," she said. "It's about music."

"Music?"

"Classical music."

Oh.

We got off the elevator on the seventh floor, and I pointed her the way down the corridor to the feature department, where the arts and entertainment writers are located.

"You don't really look like a model," I tried again.

She smiled a little. "Oh? Then what?"

"Uh . . . a musician. Strictly classical."

She sort of laughed a little then. "This way?" she asked, glancing toward Features.

"Maybe I'd better show you."

So I walked her into Features and found Patti Harrison, who writes about entertainment and recitals and painting exhibitions and what-have-you.

"Patti, this is . . ." I paused, smiling at my waterfall vision and waiting for her to say her name.

"Ariel Ryan."

I let the fresh breeze of her name wash over me. Ariel Ryan. Ah, me, sometimes a vision appears and there are no imperfections whatsoever.

Ariel told Patti all about the Mozart String Quartet, of which she was a member, and how they were playing a series of concerts on Sunday nights at St. Randolph's Church and needed an item in the *Daily Press*. What they actually needed, of course, was an item in *The New York Times*, which is more of a classical music paper than we are, but when you play in a string quartet and you do not have Itzhak Perlman with you, you try the *Daily Press*, too. Anyway, Patti stood there listening to Ariel with one ear and looking at me at the same time, trying to figure out whether Ariel was a contract or had just wandered in off the street. She saw right away I was interested, so she eventually managed to squeeze in a snippet about the concerts among her other items about Mel Torme and Bobby Short.

Anyway, so that's how I met Ariel. Of course, Patti Harrison couldn't put the item in immediately, which is what people always expect with newspapers. So Ariel called me at the paper and asked if I knew when the item was going to be in, and when I said I didn't know, she asked if I could nudge Patti. This required me to meet with Ariel to go over it, which meant going over Ariel as far as I was concerned.

"Why don't we have a drink?" I suggested slyly.

"Well, all right."

"Where would I find you after work?"

"At the Broadway Theatre."

"You're seeing a Broadway show? What's playing there?"

" 'Les Miserables' is playing there, and I'm not seeing it. I'm doing it."

"You're in the Pit?"

"With all the other miserable fiddlers." She laughed.

Like Erik Halvorsen, Ariel also played in the pit at Broadway musicals and in various orchestras and elsewhere. She also had a few young students including one, Dennis Hanley from Queens, who was concertmaster for the Metropolitan Youth Symphony Orchestra, a collection of the best high school musicians in the New York area who gave concerts at Carnegie Hall. I picked her up after the show at the stage door of the Broadway Theatre at

53rd and Broadway, and we walked down to Charlies on West 45th Street. We sat at a table in the bar, and she gave me a sort of puzzled smile.

"You're my first reporter," she said.

"Well, I never fiddled around with a violin player before."

She gave me the kind of glance that said the joke was already stale when Apollo was strumming a lyre. Ariel was sort of wistful, distant. But sometimes she would reach across the table and touch my hand and give me such a smile that I felt I needed a change of oil.

When Patti told me the item was going to be in the next day, I took a proof of it along with me and showed it to Ariel. There was the usual reaction: she oohed and aahed over it and then wondered why it wasn't bigger. We were sitting at a table in the bar at Charlies when Hally came in to have a look. He was quite tickled, too. Then he noticed the item didn't include the address. Ah, well.

She introduced Halvorsen as the quartet manager who had booked them into St. Randolph's. A manager, it turned out, is a musician who hires other musicians and handles the business side of things. Hally had organized the Mozart String Quartet and the St. Randolph's job was his first flight.

Hally gave the impression that this first outing was only the beginning of what he believed would be a meteoric rise. Ariel gave the impression that she considered Hally to be a balloon with too much air in it.

Right away, I knew there was electricity between them. Whether negative or positive, I couldn't tell.

"This is Ed Fitzgerald," she told him. "He's with the *Daily Press*."

Hally's alert, gray eyes opened wider. "Critic?"

Ariel laughed.

"Just a reporter," I told him.

"Oh." He seemed disappointed. That's the way it is

when people meet a reporter. If they're a quarterback they assume you're a sportswriter. If they're a musician they think you must be a critic. If they're a politician, they don't care what you are.

"You got a card?" Hally asked me.

"I told you he isn't a critic," Ariel said.

I dug out one of my cards for him anyway. I almost never have any with me, but on that night I had a few because Bobby the head copy boy had come around handing out boxes of them that had just been printed up. The *Daily Press* liked us to carry cards around with us as though we were all journalists, but mostly we threw them in our desk drawers and there they sat.

We went through the usual small talk. I told Hally I covered murders and other extracurricular activities, and he said he was concertmaster of the orchestra at "The Phantom of the Opera," which is the first violinist under the conductor.

But, he added quickly, he didn't expect to be that much longer. "I expect to be the contractor on the next Broadway show I'm with."

"I thought you were dumping Broadway altogether," offered Ariel.

"Patience." From the side of his mouth. "I'm willing to be contractor for a show or two."

"Imagine," said Ariel. "He's willing. And after that, I suppose, it's the Philharmonic?"

"Who knows?" he smiled. "I don't intend to be a fiddler all my life. All I need is a little capital."

"Ah, yes, capital!" Ariel floated her head around. "And what's the latest get-rich scheme?"

Hally grinned, half defensively, half mysteriously. "I'm working on something just a shade better than stupendous," he said.

"Oh? Gun-running?" More electricity.

"How about a Stradivarius?"

"How about it?"

"I've located one, and I might have a buyer."

Ariel made an I've-heard-that-song-before face, and we talked of other things. Later, she told me that Hally was always working on some deal that would make him rich as Paganini so he would no longer have to humiliate himself playing trashy Broadway show music in the pits.

"I like Broadway music," I told her.

"You would." But she gave me a poignant smile as though saying she would overlook this aberration.

So, that Sunday I went around to St. Randolph's and listened to the Mozart String Quartet weaving its tapestry. Ordinarily, I'm not too crazy about string quartet music, which becomes sort of monotonous. I think the musicians enjoy it more than the listeners. I much prefer Ella Fitzgerald singing Cole Porter, but of course I didn't tell Ariel that.

Afterward, the quartet and I walked a couple of blocks over to the Algonquin Hotel on West 44th Street, and crowded into the little bar off the lobby. Hally was with Ingrid Sohn, the quartet's violist, a dark-haired, intense woman with squinting eyes, and Mitchell Rogers, another contractor violinist who knew them all.

We all squeezed against the back wall of the bar: Hally, Ingrid, and Mitch; Ariel and I; Mark Cohen the cellist, pudgy with an amiable Bugs Bunny smile; and his large, loud wife. There were a couple others, too. All musicians or friends, apparently.

Hally announced that his first action as a new contractor would be to pay for everything.

"My party," he said happily.

Well, everybody seemed to think that was remarkable.

"Good God!" Mark Cohen the cellist whooped, "Hally's buying!" He waved an arm at Rogers. "Look out, Mitch," he chirped. "Hally's moving in on you everywhere."

This remark caused general hilarity among the Mozart String Quartet, and a flush rose in Mitch Rogers's face.

Ingrid Sohn gave Cohen a flinty glare and hissed, "I think your strings are too tight, Mark—or is it your shorts?"

Hally pretty much held court that night, tossing money around from a stuffed wallet and showing off what he assured everybody was a genuine Stradivari violin.

Mitch Rogers looked at it intently. "My God, is that really a Strad?" he said enviously.

"Look at it!" Hally beamed, getting respect.

Well, currents went back and forth and I couldn't sort them out just then. But I had to believe Hally and Ariel had once been an item. Now it appeared that he was with Ingrid Sohn—or was trying to be, because she seemed to have eyes for Mitch Rogers. Actually, it was a triangle, but I didn't know it then.

Later I asked Ariel if the violin Hally was showing off was really a Strad.

"Of course not," she said.

I was on general assignment for the *Daily Press*, covering murders, jewel robberies, trials, and other routine catastrophes under Ironhead Matthews, our excitable city editor. Ironhead had been slugged with a nightstick while covering a riot as a young reporter, and had been trying to get even with the world ever since.

Sometimes I wondered whether Ariel was attracted by my admittedly indefinable wonders or if she only wanted me to get stories in the paper about her musical endeavors. Because even after Patti printed a snippet about the Mozart String Quartet, Ariel kept after me to get something printed in the main sheet.

I stood at the city desk, under the big four-sided clock attached to the ceiling, shuffling my feet like a schoolboy.

"Uh, Ironhead, could you use a short about the Mozart String Quartet?"

Ironhead chomped on his slimy cigar and glared up at me, his neck crooked to hear better what I had said. "What?"

"See, this group is really terrific, and they're doing concerts at St. Randolph's Church on Park Avenue."

"Concerts?"

"I could even get you some free tickets."

"Is this a gag?" he wanted to know. When I explained that it wasn't, he told me in boldfaced italic that one, concerts were handled by entertainment; that two, I was not an entertainment writer and the very conception was unfathomable; and that three, he was busy handling real, hard news and had no time to listen to brazen requests for free publicity from reporters who wanted to promote their Aunt Tilly from Bensonhurst.

"It's not my aunt," I said, and got the cold, yellow-eyed stare of a lion on the Serengeti Plain selecting a wildebeest for its dinner.

"If you want to get one of your second-rate fiddlers into the paper, have him jump under an A train," he finished.

It wasn't until I got the word about Erik Halvorsen that Ironhead's words struck me. Erik hadn't gone under an A train, but he was just as dead as if he had.

2

I CAME HOME late that Monday night to my place on East 82nd Street after an endless day covering a prison riot at the Queens Annex Men's House of Detention in Long Island City. We had drawn straws to see who would go inside and talk to the rioting prisoners, and I had "won." I had gone through the flooded corridors and into the big, open prison yard where smashed glass windows hung in shards and the prisoners all stood around screaming, wearing towels around their faces like Arabs, both to hide their faces and because of the tear gas.

I was beat when I got home, and felt grubby all over, so I was in the shower when the phone rang. It was the West 10th Street police station in the Village.

"Edward Fitzgerald?" came this cop's voice.

"Yes."

"Daily Press?"

All I needed was for one of those deranged Arab inmates to insist that I come back out to the Men's Annex and listen to a list of prisoner demands.

"Yeah," I admitted tiredly.

"You know a man named Erik Halvorsen?" he asked then, and I drew a blank in my groggy state.

"Who?"

"You don't know him?"

"That skel who's in for murdering his drug dealer?" I asked, trying to separate the sea of howling faces I had looked at all day in the Men's Annex.

Now the cop was lost. "Murder? This guy's wanted in a homicide?"

"Wait a minute," I said, getting plugged in at last. "Erik Halvorsen, did you say . . . the violinist?"

"Is he a violinist?"

I rubbed my eyes and wished I could collapse in bed.

"I know him, I guess," I told the cop.

"You guess?"

"All right. I know him. Why?"

"We found one of your cards among his effects."

Wonderful words cops use.

"Did something happen to him?" I tried again.

"You want to come down here?" the cop asked, still not giving anything away.

I put in a quick call to Ariel Ryan after that, and she came on the phone in a state of gaspy anxiety.

"It's Fitz," I told her. "I just got a call from the cops about Hally."

"Oh my god," she managed.

"Do you know what happened?"

No, she said, only that something was terribly wrong. The cops had called Mitch Rogers, the contractor who had hired Erik Halvorsen for "The Phantom of the Opera," and Mitch had called her. She had been trying to reach me all day.

"Where does he live?" I asked her.

Ariel gave me Erik's address, down on West 11th Street in Greenwich Village, and his phone number.

"I'll see what I can find out," I told her.

Then I put in a call to Hally's apartment down in the Village, and a cautious man answered.

"Hello?"

The tone of voice and the single word wasn't supposed to offer any hint of who was talking or what might be going on there, but I knew both things right away.

"Listen, this is Ed Fitzgerald, *Daily Press*."

The voice opened up at that, but not in welcome. Annoyance.

"What, already?" The phone clunked, and I heard the cop's voice saying, "Hey, Wilson . . . the press."

Then another voice came onto the line. "Detective Wilson."

"Hi, Wilson. Fitzgerald, *Daily Press*. What's cooking?"

"Oh, yeah," he said. "You're the one whose card he was using?"

That's the way it is with cops. They answer all your questions with questions of their own. And since I'm a reporter, I do the same thing.

"What?"

"How well did you know this guy?"

"How about telling me what happened?" I came right back.

Wilson was silent for a moment. "Nobody told you yet?"

"Not exactly."

"Homicide."

A spasm went through me when I heard that casual word. I had suspected it all right when that first cop called and said my card was in Hally's "effects." But this made it official.

"How'd it happen?" I asked.

"We'll get to that," came Wilson's soft, official words.

"I'm on my way," I told him.

"No, no. Wait a minute."

I hung up.

You know how it is when you're so tired you feel your consciousness starts about halfway up your nose, and above that it's all caked ice? That's the way I felt walking to the blue 1978 Monte Carlo I was driving. It's as though there's an elevator inside your head trying to go up but it's stuck about two-thirds of the way to the top. Above that, where you're supposed to think, there's fog swirling around over the caked ice.

I climbed into the Monte Carlo, after fighting to get the damned door open as usual, and headed downtown on Second Avenue. There were still wispy, acrid whiffs of stench from the burning, disinfected Queens Annex House of Detention lingering in my head, and I was trying to get the elevator to climb above it so I could make sense of things.

I drove down Second Avenue, down across 42nd Street, past the *Daily Press* building, with its blinking sign giving the temperature in Celsius and Fahrenheit and then alternating by blinking the time on and off. Seven forty-two P.M. You keep on heading downtown to 14th Street, and then across Manhattan to the West Side, and then downtown again on Seventh Avenue into Greenwich Village.

Manhattan is a pretty easy place to find your way around, as long as you're above 14th Street. Because basically it's a huge grid, with one-way avenues going north and south and one-way streets going east and west, the odd-numbered ones west and the even ones east. The main crosstown streets are two-way: 14th and 23rd, and 34th, and 42nd.

But when you get south of 14th Street, down in the Village, there's no grid. The streets developed out of cowpaths when the city grew steadily northward from the original settlement below Wall Street. Wall Street was a real wall across the lower tip of Manhattan once, to keep the Indians out or the old New Amsterdam burghers in, or maybe both.

Anyway, in the Village the streets go slantwise and they're narrow and crowded, which is supposed to be quaint, I guess, unless you're driving a sloping blue Monte Carlo that's too damned wide and long for cowpaths.

Down Seventh to Greenwich Avenue and then west across West 11th Street to the old brick five-story walkup where Hally had his apartment.

Inside, there was a huge gloomy hallway and iron steps,

13

of course, hugging the wall upward. I plodded up the stairs to the fourth floor and found a uniformed cop standing in the hallway.

"Fitzgerald, *Daily Press*."

The cop gave me a glance and let out a breath.

Past the cop and to the door of Halvorsen's apartment. It was one of those crazy Village places where there's a room stuck off a corridor, and then a squeezed-in, tiny kitchen, and then a couple of other larger rooms. By larger I don't mean big. Manhattan apartments are not big, unless you live on the upper West Side or maybe in a penthouse somewhere.

Detective Wilson looked at me as I came in.

"Fitzgerald?"

I nodded.

He was a thick-bodied, short man with a moon face and a hairpiece, wearing a pretty loud sport jacket that looked like something Jackson Pollock might have designed by dripping red and green paint all over it.

"I got a call from the station," I told him.

"Well, why didn't you go there?" he wanted to know, which was ridiculous. A reporter goes to the scene.

Wilson looked away grumpily and then back at me. "You covering this story?" he asked.

"I don't know," I said. "I guess so. Why?"

He frowned, and didn't seem to like that much. "Because you seem to be part of this thing, and maybe there's a conflict of interest."

"What do you mean?" I complained. "I just gave the guy my card, that's all."

"So you know him, then?"

"Not really."

"You give your card to strangers?"

"Sure. Who else?"

"What'd he want with it?"

"He thought I was a music critic."

Toupee Wilson gave me a funny look. "Are you?"

"No."

"Well," he said, squaring himself to give me a challenging look, "I don't want you on the scene until I decide whether you're part of the case."

"*You* don't want?" I exploded. "Since when does the police department assign reporters to stories?"

"It may be a story to you, but it's a homicide case to me," he came right back. "And if you want anything about it, you'll have to go through the P.I. office downtown."

I lighted a Tiparillo as we stood in the doorway, and decided to try sweet reason. "Look, Wilson, I'm not trying to screw up your detail," I told him. "I met the guy a couple of times. If he was using my card, I'm interested."

"Who said he was using your card?"

"You did."

Wilson muttered something obscene, stood aside, and nodded his head for me to enter. "Come on in here." I went in, across the little hall that apparently led to the living room toward the front, which he was blocking off from me, and came into the tiny kitchen. The place was a shambles. Broken dishes lay on the floor and in the sink. Cupboard doors stood open, and a box was on the floor, sugar spilling out of it.

"What happened here?" I asked, giving the place a quick glance.

Wilson didn't seem to hear me. "I don't know about this," he said, and sat at a tiny round wooden table wedged into a corner. I sat, too.

"Suppose you fill me in on what you know about the deceased." I realized he meant Erik Halvorsen, who had become a crime exhibit, past tense.

I told him about meeting Erik and giving him my card. I didn't see any reason to mention Ariel Ryan. He sat there bent over, taking notes in his little notebook with a Flair pen, and I watched his hairpiece bob up and down.

15

"So, he was a professional violinist?"

"Yes."

"Hmmmmm."

There wasn't a lot Wilson could tell me, he said. Somebody had shot Erik Halvorsen inside his apartment sometime after midnight. It could have been 2 or 3 A.M., because nobody reported hearing shots. Somebody who had been telephoning Erik all day finally called the police at about 4 P.M. and asked them to check the apartment.

"We found him about five," Wilson concluded.

"Who tipped you?" I asked.

Wilson looked right at me and said nothing.

"Were they after his violin?" I tried again.

Detective Wilson smoothed down his toupee and put his notebook and Flair pen away. "I told you, you'll have to go through downtown."

"What? After I told you everything, you're going to dummy up on me?"

Wilson stood up. "You've got a conflict of interest here, Fitzpatrick—"

"Fitzgerald."

"You tell your paper to assign somebody else to this story. And I want a full statement from you."

I looked a hole through him. "Listen, Wilkins, if you have any more questions, you can go through my city desk!"

"Now, just a minute—"

I stormed through the door but went the wrong way and found myself in the living room.

"Get outa there!"

But it was too late. It was one of those old, plaster-wall rooms with a light fixture in the ceiling with three twirled cone-shaped, vanilla-colored bulbs in it and no shade. There was Erik, sprawled on his back on the sofa, his chest a mass of blood. I remembered with a swift, merciless stab of horror the time I was driving on the FDR Drive and a dog came frisking out over the wall onto the drive and under the wheels of my car. That frozen pinpoint of anguish never leaves me for long, and neither does the sight of Erik and the bloody chest.

"Christ," I muttered, and looked away.

"Several shots," Wilson said professionally. "From pretty close up."

Wilson didn't seem too upset that I'd seen the body. Maybe he thought the sight would loosen my tongue. I felt it was about to loosen my stomach.

"As long as you've seen the body, can you identify him?" he asked then.

"Yeah," I managed.

"Who is it?"

"Erik Halvorsen," I said.

"Okay," he said. "That'll do for a tentative ID till I can reach the next of kin. And that makes you a witness in this case."

I glanced one last time. The glittering eyes were lifeless now, and there was that total immovability of the dead. There's the quick and there's the dead, and you don't have to look twice to tell the difference.

The living room and the little dining room off it—it was really all one room with a sort of arch between—were in incredible chaos. Books and music sheets all over the floor, pictures and posters torn off the wall. It was as though a shell had hit it.

Then I saw Erik's violin case in the little dining room, on a small table beside a music stand. The case was open, with the cover lying back against the wall. His violin was in plain sight.

"So they didn't get the fiddle," I said.

Wilson said nothing, or if he did I didn't hear him. The walls were closing in on me. I walked out of there in a hurry, down the iron staircase and out the door onto 11th Street, gulping in air. The constricted feeling in my chest

17

wasn't from the Men's House of Detention anymore.

I walked across Hudson Street and into the White Horse Tavern on the corner, where the Welsh poet Dylan Thomas used to hang out. Dylan, they say, once made a glass pyramid of drinks on the bar at the White Horse at a time when he had been told to stop drinking or die. He drank them all up.

I called the *Daily Press* and got Rick Mazzili, the night city editor.

"Fitz here. Listen, I seem to have come across a murder."

"Yeah? A good one?"

Rick was all business, of course. There are routine murders and good ones, and that's the way you look at murder in New York if you're a newspaperman.

"So-so," I had to say. In times like that, you operate on automatic pilot. "He was a fiddle player for a Broadway show."

"Might not be too bad," said Rick, and I heard him yelling to Rafferty to take some notes.

"A fiddle player, huh?" Rafferty asked when he came on the phone.

"Yeah. Hey, Raf, look, the guy also played at Carnegie Hall. Call him a violinist, will you?"

3

IT WASN'T UNTIL I was phoning the story in that I remembered about the violin's supposedly being a Stradivarius. Because of the upheaval in my stomach when I looked at Erik's bloody chest, I had neglected to check that with Wilson. The way it is in the newspaper business, a Stradivarius is even more important than a dead body, simply because there are a lot more dead bodies in New York than Stradivari violins and Strads are probably worth more.

It's always a temptation to use such angles, but there is also the nagging possibility that it might not be true. Erik had said it was a Strad, but Ariel had said it wasn't. I had no independent knowledge. A saying from James Gordon Bennett of the old *New York Herald* popped into my mind:

"Remember this: many a good story has been ruined by oververification."

It was a lot better story with a Stradivarius. And if the *Post* or the *Times* later confirmed it was a Strad and used it, Ironhead would claw my stomach out. That's the trouble with titillating but unverified "facts"—there's always the danger that the opposition will use it, and then your stomach will be clawed out because you didn't use it, even if it turns out later that the fact was wrong.

Finally, I virtuously overcame the temptation and dashed back across West 11th Street to check it out with Detective Wilson. But a sergeant told me he had left.

"You that reporter?" he asked.

"Yeah. You know where he went?"

The sergeant looked me over. "He wanted to talk to you. He wants you down at the squad to give a statement."

Great. I was supposed to get my story from P.I. downtown, but he wanted a statement.

"Okay," I told him, and left. He'd get his statement when I was ready. I had other fish to fry.

It was bad enough looking at Erik's bloody chest; now I had to drive uptown and talk to Ariel Ryan. What do you say at such times?

"One man after burying another is laid out dead, and another buries him," reflects Marcus Aurelius. "And all this in a short time. In conclusion, observe how ephemeral and worthless human beings are, and how what was yesterday a little juice, tomorrow will be a mummy or ashes."

Of course my ancient Roman mentor was correct that the death of anyone is inevitable and insignificant in the great galactic scheme of things, but it is of little comfort to the living to point out that they too will be ashes soon enough.

So as I drove uptown I pondered the Aurelian maxim for myself and tried to think of other words for Ariel. From 11th Street in the Village, you head west across 14th Street to the West Side Highway and then north along the Hudson River, past the permanently docked aircraft carrier U.S.S. Intrepid at 43rd Street and on up the Henry Hudson Parkway to 79th Street.

Ariel lived up on Riverside Drive at 91st Street in one of those old, stone mansions that have been converted into apartment buildings. You go up three steps and into a glass square just inside, where the doorman looks you over and lets you into the lobby. Then up in a slowly moving elevator, and knock gently on her door.

"Yes?" she cried out.

"It's Fitz."

The door opened a crack and she peeked out and then flung it wide. I went in and she was in my arms, trembling like a kitten. She clung to me like that, her head buried in my chest. She was wearing cut-off jeans and her feet were bare, and she seemed to me considerably more than "a little juice," as Marcus had suggested. Finally, she moved away and walked into her living room, a high-ceilinged place overlooking Riverside Park and the Drive. I followed.

She walked to a red-lacquered table at the end of a lived-in looking sofa and stood there lighting a cigarette, her hands and arms moving as gracefully as if she were drawing a bow across her violin to play the opening high thin parabola of *Scheherazade*.

She looked at me, her eyelids fluttering to keep back the tears trembling behind them, and said nothing. She hadn't asked me a thing about Erik, but she knew. It was as though she didn't want me to say it, as though Erik would be still alive as long as nothing were said.

But then her rigid hear-no-evil posture slid away, and she sank down onto the sofa and drew her bare feet up under her.

"Is it true?" she finally asked.

I nodded my head.

"I just can't believe it." Her left hand was over her eyes. "Not Hally."

Marcus Aurelius's words flitted into my consciousness and then out again.

"Why would anyone do this?" she finally said, looking at me in bewilderment, appealing for help.

I lighted a Tiparillo. "I don't know," I said. "I would have said somebody was after his violin. But it wasn't even taken."

Then something else occurred to me.

"He had a lot of money on him," I said. "Did you see him pay for everything? Maybe it was the money. Damn! I forgot to ask the cops. Let me call the detective."

But Ariel looked stricken. "Oh, God, Fitz, don't get involved," she whimpered. And she was crying.

I wanted to tell her that I seemed to be already about as involved as I could get, short of being the corpus delicti. But I didn't call. Ariel needed me, and that was all I could think of. She shrank back into herself, a frightened, vulnerable ball of trembling. "It isn't possible to live in this city," she raged helplessly. "You can't carry anything on the streets. You can't even walk on the streets. Remember that girl they killed at the Met?"

What could I say? I understood her feeling that "they" were out there killing people, some roving band of savages who were somehow all connected together in one vast army of thugs.

"I've been robbed right here twice," she went on. "And my girlfriend Lynn—she was walking into the building right in front and they grabbed her purse from a car and drove up the street and dragged her three blocks because her arm was caught in the purse strap."

Anybody who lives in New York has war stories to tell.

"Yeah, I know," I muttered helplessly. "What a city."

"Why do we live here?" she appealed to me. "I've got to get out!"

I paced around, feeling just as helpless, and came face-to-face with a stainless-steel framed poster on the wall about a Gustav Mahler concert at Lincoln Center. I didn't know what else to say. I sometimes wondered, too, why we stayed in the crazy minefield of New York.

"What happened?" she finally asked in a muted monotone.

She was ready to hear the details, but I wasn't ready to give them. I found myself thinking of Detective Wilson's being unwilling to tell me anything. Now I felt like that. She didn't need to know about Erik's bloody chest.

I sank into a stuffed chair under the Mahler poster.

"Somebody shot him."

She closed her eyes and shriveled up even more.

"Do they have any idea who it might have been?" she asked numbly.

"No." I was just as flat.

"Of course not," she said listlessly.

"I keep wondering, Ariel, do you think Hally really had a Stradivarius?" I said.

"Well, I didn't think so before," she said hesitantly.

"What would one be worth?"

She wagged her head. "I don't know. Plenty. There was a story about one being auctioned off in London last week for three hundred thousand dollars."

"See, that might be a reason," I suggested.

"But you said the violin wasn't even taken."

Yes, that was true. But when a person walks around with a quarter-million-dollar violin and turns up dead, you want to know about that violin. In newspaper stories and in murders, which are often the same thing, you always go for the most obvious.

"If he did have one," I pressed on, "where could he have gotten it? I didn't even know you could buy them."

"Oh, yes," she said. "You can buy them. Not fiddle players, of course, but . . . somebody . . ." She trailed off.

She was sitting up a little, trying to think. She was ready enough to try to think about violins, rather than about Erik.

"Where did he buy his own fiddle?"

"LaPorte's," she said quickly. "Charles LaPorte, on West Fifty-Seventh Street, across from Carnegie Hall. A lot of us go there, for strings and repairs and things."

"Does he handle Stradivaris?"

Ariel gestured uncertainly. "I never shopped for one myself, but I would think so."

I went over and sat by her on the sofa, and she cuddled against me. It was odd, but Erik's death was knocking down barriers. Maybe it wasn't so odd. When somebody you know dies, you realize you have only so much time, and you wonder if you're living your only life the way you really want to.

Ariel snuggled against me, her face in my neck. Having a lovely woman in your arms also makes you think. When you're a reporter in New York, it sometimes seems as though the only life you have is your job. You meet a woman, and the job comes between you. Not because you want it to. It just does. It somehow always comes to a point where you have to choose one or the other, and what you really need is both.

"Thanks for coming, Fitz," she told me. "God, I needed you tonight."

We held each other that night, and things were different after that. I wasn't just a reporter following a story day by day anymore. I was a man in love, wondering for the first time in a long time about a dangerous and fickle thing called the future.

4

You might have seen the story about Hally's murder in the *Daily Press* the next day. You might have missed it, too, because it wasn't much: a few graphs on page nine. Without the Stradivarius angle, it was just another murder, and just another murder in New York isn't much in the way of news.

When I got to the office the next morning, there was a message from Detective Wilson. Wanting a statement, no doubt. I put in a call to the Sixth Precinct detective squad down on West 10th Street, and right away he wanted to know why I had fled from the scene of the crime.

"Nervous tummy?" he asked, with what I imagined was a smartass-cop smile.

"Something like that."

"I need a statement," he went on. "Why don't you come on down here and let's go over it." He seemed a little more friendly, now that I had something he wanted.

Ironhead Matthews didn't have anything hot for me, so I told him I'd try to find a follow on the violin murder. "The guy supposedly had a Stradivarius," I made the mistake of saying.

"What?" snapped Ironhead, grabbing the paper. "I don't see that in your story."

"No, I'm not sure yet."

"Well, did you ask?" he wanted to know.

"See, it wasn't taken."

"The guy's got a Stradivarius, and it wasn't taken?" Ironhead was giving me a challenging stare. That was an

25

even better story, he suggested.

"I'll find out," I told him.

"Okay," he said. "And I want that angle."

Terrific. Me and my big mouth. Now I had a Stradivarius in the story, and I didn't even know if there was one.

I walked back to the library and checked out the clips on Stradivari violins, about which I knew approximately nothing beyond the name. Sooner or later, when you're covering a story, you have to figure out what it's all about. I stuffed the clipping envelope into my jacket pocket and headed down to the NYP parking zone on East 40th Street to my Monte Carlo. It wasn't in the mood to move that day, which wasn't unusual.

Arunga-runga-runga, it went, before finally spluttering to life. One day, I knew, it would refuse to move at all. There's something about driving a car in Manhattan that brings out the worst in them. Potholes, probably. Anyway, it makes no sense to drive an expensive car in Manhattan on a daily basis, which is why I've gone through a series of clunkers—that and because I could never get ahead enough to buy a new car.

I headed down the FDR Drive to 14th Street, and then across town into the Village and to the West 10th Street station. Upstairs to the squad room with a cup of coffee, and there I found Detective Theodore H. Wilson at his desk smoothing down his toupee. He wasn't wearing his Jackson Pollock jacket, but he had on a green shirt with a blue tie. I suddenly got the idea he must be color-blind.

I plunked down beside his desk, opened my coffee, lighted a Tiparillo, and said, "Well, am I still a suspect?"

Wilson's face got a little red. "Listen, I just do my job."

"Me too."

"All right, all right," he grumbled. "I just don't want a lot of stuff printed when I'm trying to clear this damned thing up."

"Did you see the story today?"

"Yeah, yeah, that was okay," he said grudgingly.

Sure, I thought. There was practically nothing in it.

"So, what else can you tell me about this case?" he said.

I filled him in on the concert at St. Randolph's, and about going to the Algonquin bar afterward. He wanted to know who was there, and I went down the list with him again. He took down all the names, Mitch Rogers the contractor, Ingrid Sohn, Mark Cohen and his wife, Ariel, and me.

"I left with Ariel, and they all went their separate ways," I told him.

"Hmmmmm."

"Did you ever figure out whether anything was taken?" I asked. "Did they get his money?"

"What money?"

"He had some in his wallet, quite a lot."

"How do you know that?" said Wilson.

"He bought drinks, and everybody must have seen it."

"Hmmmmm." As always, one of his most enlightening remarks.

"What I don't get is why whoever it was didn't take the violin," I told him. "It's supposed to be a Stradivarius."

"What?" That interested him.

"Erik's fiddle. He told us it was a Stradivarius."

"He told who that?"

"Everybody. And he showed it, too."

"We've got it in the property clerk's office," he said. "We'll check that out. I don't want that mentioned now."

"What do you mean?" I complained. "That's the whole angle."

"It isn't an angle if it isn't a Stradivarius, is it?" he came back.

"Well . . . no."

"I'll let you know."

"Any ideas?" I asked.

27

Wilson put down his Flair pen and put both hands on top of his head as though thinking, but really to smooth down his toupee.

"Well, I don't know," he said brilliantly. "Was this guy carrying this Stradivarius?"

"Yes, as far as I know."

"Hmmmmm."

And that was that, for the moment. I heard later that Wilson brought in everybody for questioning during the next two days, for which they blamed me, naturally. I guess I was to blame, actually, since I'd given him their names, but it was really the fault of the person who killed Erik and started the whole thing. But people don't think that way.

I left Wilson to his search for witnesses, and possibly the killer, and went on my own quest for the Stradivarius. I fell into a hole-in-the-wall coffee shop on the corner, got some coffee and took out the clippings.

The stories were mostly about how Stradivari violins had been sold at Sotheby's or Christie's auction houses for steadily ascending rates. One of the stories apparently was the one Ariel mentioned. A Strad had sold recently in London for $300,000.

The background was that one Antonio Stradivari had once toiled long and hard and well in Cremona, Italy, near Milan, making fine violins until he was about ninety years old. He had died in 1737, which meant that any of his instruments still around were something like two hundred and fifty years old. I had to think there couldn't be many of them left, and that they were antique works of art rather than violins actually in use.

As Ariel had said, Charles LaPorte's place was on West 57th Street across from Carnegie Hall, on the twelfth floor. There was his listing in the lobby directory, with a drawing of a violin beside it. "Charles LaPorte, luthier." I concluded a luthier was a violin maker or dealer. I rode up in the elevator and found a door with another violin on it.

Inside, there was a large high-ceilinged room with shiny violins hanging on the walls and more of them in velvet boxes in glass cases around the room. I walked over to a woman at a typewriter. The sign on her desk said WILMA MANNING.

"I'm looking for Mr. LaPorte," I told her.

"Mr. LaPorte!" she called out, without even looking up.

And here came Charles LaPorte, walking along behind the counter toward me, smiling like a French Minister of Culture.

"Yes?" A darkly handsome gentleman of middle years with carefully styled black hair and a nervous, blinking tick in his alert eyes.

"Hello," I said. "Ed Fitzgerald, *Daily Press*."

The alert eyes blinked rapidly, and Charles LaPorte smiled invitingly.

"Well," he said, "hello! What can I do for ze *Daily Press*?"

"I don't know," I said. "Do you know Erik Halvorsen?"

A slight frown crossed LaPorte's gallic features. "Ze violinist?"

"Yes."

LaPorte sort of nodded. "I know Erik. Why?"

I couldn't tell whether LaPorte knew about Erik's death or not. But he seemed to react to his name, all right.

"Have the police been here?" I offered.

"What! Police?" A tremolo of blinks. LaPorte's right arm rose, floated uncertainly, and then fell. "No! What 'as 'appened?"

Apparently he *didn't* know about Erik. But he was strung as tightly as an A string, nevertheless.

"They will be," I told him. "Somebody shot Erik."

I thought Charles LaPorte was going to faint. His eyes widened and he swayed behind the counter.

"*Mon Dieu!*" he gasped.

I let it sink in for a moment. It appeared to sink in all the

29

way down into LaPorte's trim stomach.

"But . . . why would zey come to me?" he finally managed.

"Well, you did business with him, didn't you?"

The arms come up and fling out on both sides. He might be about to start conducting an orchestra. "I sell 'im a violin. I glue it when 'e sits on it. *Voilà*."

"He sat on his violin?"

Blink go the eyes. "I do not know where Mr. Halvorsen sits. It might have been Zubin Mehta, *hein*? I glue all ze same."

"Do you know anything about Stradivari violins?"

"Stradivari . . . ? Do *I* know about Stradivari? Do you know who you are talking to, monsieur?"

I had to admit I didn't know. "I understand Erik was looking for one, and—"

"Poof, poof, poof! Everybody ees looking for one."

"Well, but I understand Erik actually found one," I said.

LaPorte looks and doesn't blink. "Yes. So?"

Something has happened. The inviting welcome I received upon entering has fled. The news of Erik's death nudged it into motion. The mention of the police sent it in hasty flight.

I studied my trembling Frenchman and took out a Tiparillo.

"What ees zat?"

"What?"

"You may not light zat sing here!"

Oh. So I just chewed on it.

But I have given LaPorte something to focus on. He can pretend to be irritated at my Tiparillo. One cannot be expected to answer the impertinent questions of an ink-stained wretch who invades the establishment of an eminent luthier with a foul cigar. I could only press on.

"I'm trying to find out where he got the violin," I say. "And I thought he might have come to you."

30

Charles LaPorte is still focused upon my cigar. He gives the impression that he is tapping his fingers impatiently on the counter, even though by now his arms are folded across his chest. He has nothing to say.

"But, if you don't deal in Stradivari violins," I offer, going fishing.

"Don' deal in . . . !" The arms unfold. "Of course I deal in zem."

"You have Strads for sale?" I asked.

Annoyance radiated from Charles LaPorte. If he were a bomb, his fuse would be burning. He glared at me. "You 'ave no grasp of what you are talking about," he finally declared. "Zey are not stacked on a shelf like piccolos!"

I knew that was true, of course. But the only way for a reporter to find things out is to ask questions until he has a grasp. "There is no such thing as a stupid question," Ironhead liked to say. "There are only stupid answers."

"I'm just saying that if Erik wanted to get one, he wouldn't go to Sears, would he? He'd come to you, or somebody like you."

"Yes."

"I know he located a Stradivarius."

"Yes . . . well?"

I decided to take a jump in the dark. "And I happen to know he got it from you."

Charles LaPorte stopped blinking and arm-waving. He leaned across the counter anxiously. "Who told you zat?"

"The police."

He let out a breath. "*Impossible!*" I thought I had struck out, but then he shook his head. "I am a luthier, monsieur! I deal in fine violins. Amati . . . Bergonzi . . . Guarneri . . . and, yes, Stradivari. When I can get zem. *If* I can get zem. If a person comes in an' inquires, I show zem what I might be able to get. Erik ees a professional violinist. All right, so I showed 'im a Stradivarius! But showing ees not buying."

Erik had brought in his violin for refurbishing, said La-

31

Porte, and had asked about a Stradivarius.

"Erik said 'e might 'ave a buyer," said LaPorte. "And zat is all."

"Did he say who the buyer was?"

The head went back and forth energetically. "I did not take Erik too seriously."

And that was that, Charles LaPorte's manner seemed to indicate.

"So Erik didn't get a Stradivarius from you?"

"Absolutely not, monsieur," LaPorte said indignantly. He was as nervous as a lighted match in a Chinese firecracker shop.

"Mr. LaPorte, Erik was shopping a Stradivarius around for somebody, and somebody killed him for it."

LaPorte's chin trembled. "So why do you tell me zis?"

"Because whoever let Erik have that violin is out a lot of money. I'd like to help whoever it is to find the violin."

LaPorte frowned. "And your interest in ze instrument?"

"None. My interest is in where Erik got it, and where it went."

"I wish I could 'elp you," said LaPorte. He sounded as sincere as a real estate salesman.

"Well, look, if you didn't ask Erik to sell a Strad for you, do you have any idea where else he might have gotten one?"

A supercilious shrug of dismissal. How was he supposed to know that?

I reached into my jacket pocket and took out one of my *Daily Press* cards.

"Look, Mr. LaPorte, let me leave you one of my cards," I told him. "If you happen to think of where Erik might have gotten a Strad, would you give me a call?"

"But I 'ave no idea!"

He took the card, though. He was gazing at it perplexedly when I left.

5

DURING THE NEXT couple of days, I felt like Abraham Lincoln pacing around in the White House wondering what had happened to General Sherman. Sherman had left Atlanta and was marching through Georgia to the sea behind Confederate lines. Everybody knew Sherman was in Georgia somewhere, but they didn't know where until he came out at Savannah. Well, I knew my General Sherman, better known as Toupee Wilson, was marching through the witnesses in the Erik Halvorsen murder case, but I didn't know exactly where he was either.

I knew about Wilson because every time one of the Mozart String Quartet players got called in for questioning, that person would get on the phone to Ariel Ryan and chew her out for going with a big-mouth *Daily Press* reporter, and then she would call me in the city room and ask what in the world was the matter with me.

It kept me up to date on who Wilson was questioning, but it didn't give me any information to write.

And of course Ironhead was on my butt to write something, since I'd sold him on the idea that I was chasing a ring of Stradivari thieves.

"Anything on that fiddle story?" is the way he would put it anytime I got near the city desk.

"Working on it," I'd mutter.

Then the phone.

"Fitz, will you stop giving all my friends' names to the police!"

Ariel Ryan, fresh from having her ears burned off.

33

"Honey, I told you I had to give those names."

"But he keeps questioning them!"

I sighed. What did she expect a homicide detective on a murder to do, take them out for lasagna?

"They're not going to question me too, are they?" she finally asked.

"Well..."

"They *are*, aren't they! You gave them my name, too!"

"But honey..."

Slam! *Errrrrrr* ...

I dropped around to the West 10th Street detective squad room a couple of days later for a fill-in from Wilson and his partner on what they'd found out.

There sat Wilson at his desk wearing a yellow shirt and a green tie.

"When's the parade start?" I asked him.

"Parade?"

"The one you're dressed up for."

Wilson's partner, a young white-shield cop named Nickerson, looked down into his coffee carton and smiled. Wilson glanced at him, then back at me. He didn't miss much, I'll tell you that.

"Hilarious, Fitzgerald," he said sourly.

"So what'd you find out?"

"About what?"

Don't you love it when you ask somebody a perfectly obvious question and they give you a perfectly idiotic reply? About what? It was old close-mouthed Wilson again.

"Come on, Wilson. I gave you the list of people."

"Well, we didn't get much out of them," he said guardedly.

That's the way it is with cops and reporters. You go through a regular routine, and it's like a dentist talking lightly about how the Mets blew another one to the Cardinals, or how Reagan is ruining us all, when all the time he's fingering a goddam corkscrew to stab into your gums.

"You think one of the musicians got Halvorsen?" I put in.

Wilson wagged his head back and forth, unable to say.

"I don't know," he finally said. "They all can account for their movements, more or less." The Flair pen was in his hand.

"You and Ariel Ryan were together." He made a little circle. "The cello player, what's his name?" He looked at his partner Nickerson.

"Mark Cohen," said the partner.

The Flair pen made another circle around the first circle. "Mark Cohen and his wife, Sylvia—they left together and went home."

That left Mitch Rogers and Ingrid Sohn.

"Your friend the victim left with Mitchell Rogers the contractor and Ingrid Sohn," said Wilson, making more and larger concentric rings.

"Rogers drove them home," he went on. "He dropped Ingrid off at her place first." Another circle.

"Then he drove Halvorsen home and dropped him off. Then he went back to Ingrid's." Another circle.

"What was that?"

"What was what?"

"Mitch Rogers dropped Erik off and then went back to Ingrid Sohn's place?" I asked.

"That's what he said."

"Oh," I mumbled. So that apparently cleared up who Ingrid was with that night.

"Why?" said Wilson.

"Nothing. So you don't think it was anybody from the party, then?"

"It doesn't look like it," he said, retracing the target he had drawn on his pad. "Everybody can account for where they were from other people who were with them." Another target began. "Mark Cohen and his wife drove home to New Jersey, where a baby-sitter confirmed their time of arrival."

"You talked to the babysitter?"

35

"We talked to everybody."

Ariel and I had gone home, and I had been with her at her apartment for several hours, he said, glancing quizzically at me. "I talked to the doorman there," he said.

Terrific.

"Did you talk to Ariel?" I asked with trepidation.

"We did. She confirms your story. Not happily, I might add." The grinning dolt. "Ingrid Sohn confirms that Mitch came back to her place and stayed the night," he continued. "So they were together when Halvorsen was killed. That's it."

Another target was complete on his pad, but he had no one to put in the bullseye.

"This guy Mitch Rogers was the last one to see Halvorsen alive that night, but he's got an alibi: Ingrid Sohn."

Wilson dropped his Flair pen, stood up, and walked to a row of filing cabinets and back, patting his toupee.

"There's another thing, too: the violin. We've got a group of musicians here. If one of them got Halvorsen, he'd know enough to take his violin. But it wasn't taken."

"Yeah," I said. "Especially if it were a Stradivarius."

Wilson didn't answer that. He paced back to the filing cabinets again and then returned to his desk. "It doesn't figure," he concluded.

"What else have we got?"

Wilson blinked, shot a glance at Nickerson, and then looked back at me. "We?"

I ignored that. "What about the slugs?"

"Ballistics says twenty-five caliber."

"How many?"

"Six."

Six! That stopped me. "The guy shot him six times?"

"That's it."

"What do you make of that?" I asked Wilson.

There was a pause. Wilson was adjusting his toupee and

thinking it over, I decided. "Well, my guess is a punk... an amateur."

"Why?"

Because, said Wilson, the perpetrator must have kept firing until there were no more bullets, and at point-blank range.

"Maybe he wanted to make sure he was dead."

Wilson grunted. "That's what I mean. A guy who wanted to make sure he was dead, if he knew what he was doing, would have put the last four or five into his head."

A grisly picture floated before me. Big Jim Lawler of the Tenth Precinct detective squad had once detailed for me the killing of Lefty Linconetti. The killer had shot Lefty once in the chest. "That was the first shot," said Lawler, "to get his attention, you might say." And also to make Lefty helpless. Then the killer, a truly professional hit man, had gone to work. Like the killer of Erik Halvorsen, this one had emptied his weapon too.

The second and third slugs went into Lefty's eyes. The fourth and fifth had gone in Lefty's ears. The sixth had been fired upward under Lefty's chin into his brain.

I realized what Detective Wilson was telling me: it is possible to shoot somebody six times in the body and not kill him. I remembered a story I covered where a man, in fact, shot *himself* six times and finally died of shock and loss of blood. It was one of those stories where the media poked a lot of fun at the cops for calling it suicide. But it was.

"So the guy stood there blazing away till the gun was empty and then split without taking anything," I summarized.

"That's the way it looks."

"So what does it all add up to?" I asked Wilson.

He finally sat at his desk again, picked up his Flair pen and started drawing more circles within circles.

What it added up to, said Wilson, was that we had a

casual mugger committing what cops call a crime of opportunity and being scared off empty-handed.

It wasn't an unusual occurrence, Wilson explained. The mugger must have spotted Erik on the street with his violin, after Mitch Rogers dropped him off, and followed him into the building. Or maybe it was a burglar who was ransacking the apartment when Erik came in. When Erik fought him, the guy panicked, opened fire, and fled empty-handed.

"If the violin had been taken, then I might think somebody who had been at your party might have followed him home. But it wasn't taken. You saw it yourself, didn't you?"

I sighed. "Yes."

"In fact, the violin case was open." He rubbed it in. "But the killer took nothing. Scared off."

"You mean he didn't take Erik's money either?"

Wilson didn't answer that.

"How about the violin? Did you find out if it's a Stradivarius?"

Wilson remained silent on that too. I realized he kept ducking questions on both those points. Cops do that. They hold back certain information on a crime, even from reporters—especially from reporters—so there are facts that only the killer and the cops know about.

"You're not going to tell me about the money or the fiddle?"

"Listen, we got a job to do here," he answered.

Wonderful.

"What now?"

"We'll have to wait and see," said Wilson. "We've got no description on the perp . . . nothing."

There wasn't even any stolen property to try to track down. If Erik's violin had been stolen, it might turn up at a pawnshop and the shopkeeper might be able to give them a description or a lead of some kind. But this way . . . zip.

That was about all there was to it, he decided. The violin was the only thing of real value Erik had—except his life, of course. That's the way it is with a lot of professional musicians. They always have a serviceable tuxedo or evening gown and often a musical instrument worth some money, and not necessarily much more.

I let out a breath. I knew what he was saying. With no leads and no high-visibility victim, the case was on the back burner. No suspect had been apprehended, but at least the Sixth Precinct detective squad had a statement to file and an explanation to put on a report. Unless the suspect got himself arrested in some other crime and voluntarily told them about the murder, the matter was probably a dead issue.

So there it was. The mugger who had followed Erik home and emptied a .25 into his chest was home free, unless he suddenly saw a vision in church and turned himself in, an eventuality for which no odds could be calculated.

After leaving Wilson, I met Ariel for a late lunch at Charlies on West 45th Street to fill her in. We stood in the corner of the bar near the front. I had a Schaefer but she only had coffee, because she had to play "Les Miserables" that night at the Broadway Theatre. We looked at each other. I lighted a Tiparillo. We looked at each other again.

"Sorry they questioned you," I apologized.

"I guess they had to," she said softly.

Finally, I plunged in and told her what I'd gotten from Detective Wilson. She seemed resigned.

"Terrific," she said. She meant the opposite.

"Yeah."

I didn't bother to tell her about all those slugs.

"A mugger," she said in a flat voice. "Just like that. And Hally's gone."

Her words didn't seem to warrant a reply.

Standing there with Ariel, I realized that more than Hally was gone. We were gone too, unless I could find out

39

what had happened and could lay this ghost to rest. Manhattan has a way of coming between people, elbowing you apart with all the ghastliness and madness that surrounds and distracts you.

We didn't stay long. I had to get back to the office, and she had to get home to give a lesson to her star pupil, Dennis Hanley.

"He's concertmaster of the Metropolitan Youth Orchestra, and he'll do a solo at Carnegie Hall in November," she told me proudly, apparently anxious to concentrate on something—anything—else.

"You show him how," I told her.

"Oh, he doesn't need to be shown," she smiled. "He's really brilliant." She sighed. "I swear, these fabulous young string players come out of the woodwork every year."

I walked down to West 44th Street, to my blue bomb parked in the NYP zone, and drove across town to the *Daily Press*. I was feeling pretty depressed. A mugger committing a crime of opportunity. It was a fairly typical resolution of a crime in New York. That is no resolution.

That's what really drives you crazy about crime in New York—the absurd, random destructiveness of it. Roving bands of lackalls mug people on the street, sometimes maiming them for life, and then discover they have no money to steal. Or the victim causes so much trouble that they run with nothing, leaving behind only a dead body to be mourned.

A jewel thief can shoot a gem courier on West 47th Street in the diamond district and then run around the corner, duck into a subway, come back up across the street, and go back and stand across from where the cops are examining the body, and nobody even notices. A thief needs no camouflage, because the streets are jammed with people dressed every which way and nobody stands out.

For years, in the fifties and sixties, a blind giant of a man who called himself Moondog stood all day long every day on the corner of West 54th Street and Sixth Avenue wearing an army blanket and a Viking helmet with horns sticking out. He stood there motionlessly, silently, holding a staff, hoping to affront an uncaring public with his statement that proud noncooperators are always among us, a modern-day Simon Stylites. But after a while, Moondog, too, blended in with the bizarre scene of Manhattan, no more unusual than haphazardly strolling hippies and bag ladies.

Back in the office, I had to tell Ironhead I had not scored on the fiddle story.

Ironhead was at his VDT blipping away like a maniac, editing stories for the first edition. He glanced at me and nodded his head.

"Okay," he said, "forget it. Owens has a runaway car story we need right away."

So I plumped down at my desk and knocked out a story about a car that had mounted the sidewalk on 53rd Street and mowed down a crowd of pedestrians. The gas pedal had stuck, the driver said.

That's the way it is in the newspaper business. There's always another disaster to be written, and you can't spend too much time or worry over one that doesn't pan out.

By quitting time I had as good as forgotten the Halvorsen story. Wilson had kissed it off, that was for sure, and without him I had no idea of what to do, anyway.

I walked out of the city room and down to my clunker on East 40th Street, relieved in a way that it was all over. The damned door wouldn't open again. I made a mental note to have John the service station guy fix it one of these days. I had to bend over to try to yank it open, and suddenly a window in the parking garage behind me blew apart as though smashed by a baseball bat.

I half straightened up and turned around to look. And then the window next to the first one blew apart. I heard it that time: *Bang*! A sharp, quick report, like a firecracker.

A bolt of lightning went through my chest, a terrifying jab of fright, and I was down on the sidewalk beside my car.

A squeal of tires, and a million years later I looked up. A third shot had put a dent in the door on the driver's side.

6

I WISH I could tell you I jumped into my clunker and pursued the gunman through the streets of Manhattan like Stacey Keach and ran him into the East River. I wish I could tell you I at least looked up fast enough to see the damned car and write down the plate number. But the fact is I chewed a hole in the sidewalk trying to burrow into it, and would have squeezed underneath my car if I could have. Only after I was sure the car was gone did I get up and peek over the car roof. Nothing. A deserted block.

Lovely. Nobody had seen a damned thing. My legs were trembling as though I had run the New York City Marathon, and my brain was bubbling like Jello. There's nothing like a metal slug twanging past your ear to make you realize just how ephemeral a thing you are, as Marcus Aurelius had said.

I scurried along back to Second Avenue on rubber legs and hurried up to the *Daily Press*.

I beat it in through the back way, going through the loading bays past parked *Daily Press* news trucks to the freight elevator, which took a century to sway up to the seventh floor.

I burst into the city room, and Glenn the switchboard guy told me later I had ping-pong balls for eyes. I'm not surprised. My belly was full of them, too.

I sort of staggered to the city desk, collapsed into a chair across from Ironhead, and sat there like a stone. A chalky white stone.

Ironhead, who was going over the first edition page

proofs looked across at me and noticed I was about as relaxed as somebody sitting in the electric chair.

"What's the matter with you?"

I opened my mouth, but only wind came out.

"What?" he demanded.

"Somebody took a shot at me," I finally muttered.

"A shot?" He was on his feet and around the desk to me. "Where? When?"

I needed something to hold onto. A Tiparillo. Ironhead lighted it for me, which certainly showed he didn't realize what he was doing.

Only then did it come rushing out of me.

"Who was it?" Ironhead demanded. "Did you see the car?"

I shook my head.

"What's it about?" he tried again.

It was a good question. Until then, I had only thought of getting away from those blasted parking garage windows and into the safety of the city room. Now I tried to think.

Could it have been a casual mugger? Certainly. In New York that's always possible. I wasn't even sure what had happened. Apparently the gunman had driven along the street behind me, spotted me getting into my car, and opened fire. Only the fact that the idiotic door on the Monte Carlo had stuck, as usual, had caused me to bend over to tug on it, and I had ducked out of the way. Sweet, crazy, idiotic stuck door!

The gunman had fired twice more from his car and then sped off.

What did it mean? For one thing, the guy hadn't been willing to leave the safety of his car and had beat it in a hurry. So he was as terrified as I had been. I kept saying "he," but it could have been a "she," too.

"The only thing I've been working on is the fiddle story," I told Ironhead.

I'll say this for Ironhead. When something happens, *he*

happens. He knows about deadlines and doing things right now. He started yelling and stomping around, and the next thing I knew Detective Toupee Wilson and his partner Nickerson had been summoned to the *Daily Press,* and Glenn the switchboard guy had put a glass of scotch in front of me.

"Son of a bitch!" Ironhead declared.

I don't know how long it took for Wilson to get there. Time had gone telescopic on me. One second I was looking through the large end of a telescope and time was out of sight, and the next second I was at the other end and it was sitting on top of me.

And there stood Wilson frowning at me, with Ironhead at his elbow, screaming.

"Who the hell is shooting at my reporters?" he was asking.

"How the hell am I supposed to know that?" came Wilson's plaintive reply. To me he said, "What happened?"

I told him what I'd told Ironhead. That I didn't know, except that the parking garage windows behind me exploded.

"What makes you think it's about that violin?" he said then.

"What else could it be?"

"How would I know?" he said. "A lot of people might want to shoot a reporter."

Well, that didn't sit too well with Ironhead, who started carrying on about how he would not stand for marauding gunmen stalking the streets taking potshots at innocent bystanders.

"Innocent bystanders?" Wilson came back. "Your man has had his nose in this case from the beginning."

"That happens to be a reporter's job," said Ironhead.

"I've tried to tell him I don't want him covering this story," Wilson spluttered.

45

"What?" said Ironhead, and he couldn't seem to get a grip on the words. "You're trying to give orders to one of my reporters?"

"He keeps poking his nose into my case," complained Wilson.

Somebody had to, Ironhead shot back, because it was obvious that New York's Finest were wandering around like the Lost Dutchman in an impenetrable fog while some deranged killer roamed the streets blasting away at fiddlers and reporters.

Yes, said Wilson, and just what the hell was I doing to cause myself to get shot at?

He glared at me. "What the hell have you been doing?"

The moon-faced dick had invented a new crime, it seemed. Getting shot at.

"Nothing," I said, "just trying to find the Stradivarius."

"Goddammit, there is no Stradivarius in this case!" Wilson's words were cast in bronze. "Why do you keep harping on that?"

"Because I told him to." Ironhead jumped in. "Because that's the story here, if there is one."

As though from the top of the Chrysler Building, a great sigh escaped Detective Wilson.

"When are you people going to understand that this is not a *story* . . . it's a homicide investigation."

Well, that little contretemps could have easily blown up into a volcanic eruption, but then Glenn yelled over that there was an urgent call for Detective Wilson.

"Probably Internal Affairs looking to lift your gold shield!" Ironhead was livid.

It wasn't Internal Affairs, though, it was the Sixth Precinct. Wilson took the call on the city desk phone.

"Wilson," he said in his official police voice. Then he closed his eyes. "What?" Then he opened them and glared at me. "Goddammit." He let out a long breath, said, "All right," and hung up the phone.

He was looking at me again, and I had the feeling I didn't want to know why.

"I don't believe this," he said tiredly.

"What?" I asked apprehensively.

But Wilson had to roll his head around first in a great show of weariness.

"You know Charles LaPorte?"

"Who?" I said, even as I was remembering.

"Charles LaPorte. A violin dealer. Oh, you know him, all right." A touch of asperity peeked through.

"What about him," Ironhead horned in. "Whoever he is, we've got a more important matter before us here!"

Well, said Detective Theodore H. Wilson, that was a matter of opinion. There was something going on that he, Detective Wilson, was going to get to the bottom of.

"That call I got was relayed from Midtown North," he said. "You know what's in Midtown North?" He didn't bother to wait for an answer. "West Fifty-Seventh Street. You know who has an office on West Fifty-Seventh Street?" Again he wasn't interested in an answer.

"Charles LaPorte?"

He looked at me. Then at Ironhead. Then back at me.

"You've been up there asking about a Stradivarius, haven't you?"

I considered this a rather remarkable piece of clairvoyance. "Why do you say that?" I ventured.

"Because—" Wilson sighed—"you go snooping around asking people about violins, and the next thing they're dead."

"Dead?" I could barely get it out.

"Charles LaPorte has just been found dead."

My head swam.

Ironhead wasn't ready to let him get away with that flimsy circumstantial accusation, though.

"And just why do you jump to the conclusion that my reporter was up there?" he asked pugnaciously.

"Oh, no reason," said Wilson. "No reason at all. Except that the dead man has one of your reporter's cards in his hand."

There was still a finger of scotch in the glass Glenn had put in front of me. I gulped it down.

7

THE REST OF that night is a vague haze. I had been going all day, and the Schaefers I had at Charlies earlier, plus the scotch Glenn had given me, didn't help. Not to mention the exploding windows and the slug into the door of my Monte Carlo.

But none of that matters when you're on a story that blows up right in your face. There was nothing to do but walk back down to my clunker and drive up to LaPorte's.

Wilson and Nickerson had gotten there ahead of me, of course, along with a pride of blue-and-white police cars, an ambulance, and the forensics squad.

It must have been about 8 P.M by then, because there was a crowd of music lovers milling around on the sidewalk across the street in front of Carnegie Hall, waiting to go in for the concert. How nice it would be, I thought, just to walk over there and go inside and listen to something soothing like Dvorak's symphony *From the New World*. Of course, with the day I was having, the piece would probably be the *1812 Overture*, with cannons going off.

I used my press card to get past the cops at the front door of the building, and I had to show it again to get up in the elevator. Once at LaPorte's door with the violin painted on it, I ran into a problem bigger than my press card. Bigger than a bread box, too. Just about the size of a giant sour pickle.

Detective Theodore H. "Toupee" Wilson.

"Nobody home," he snapped when I tried to walk in.

"Look, Wilson, as long as we have to work together—"

Wilson's hand went up, like a traffic cop stopping a bus. "Stop right there!"

"Okay, not together. As long as we're on the same case . . ."

Wilson put his fingertips on his closed eyelids, but didn't say anything.

" . . . we might as well try to get along," I finished.

He removed his fingers, opened his eyes, and looked me over as though I were a face on a wanted poster. "Where were you when LaPorte got it?" he wanted to know.

"When did he get it?" I came right back.

The corners of Wilson's mouth went down. It was ridiculous. He was acting as though we hadn't been at the *Daily Press* together ten minutes earlier. The fact was he couldn't question me, because he didn't have any idea of what had happened. But that didn't stop him.

"When did you give LaPorte your card?" he tried again.

I told him about visiting LaPorte a few days earlier to find out if Erik Halvorsen had gotten a Stradivarius from him.

"And what did he say?"

"He said no."

He walked back through LaPorte's along the glass counters and into LaPorte's office. I followed.

There he was, slumped over his desk. As advertised, he held one of my cards in his right hand, which was lying motionless on the desktop in a puddle of blood.

Wilson surveyed the scene and muttered something. He turned to me. "Goddammit, why is it that every time I find a dead body he's got your card?"

I drew a blank.

"What links these damn murders isn't a violin, Fitzgerald. It's your cards. How do you explain that?"

I drew another blank. "Maybe it means I'm on the right track."

"What track?"

It was a good question, all right. "It's got to be the Stradivarius," I suggested.

"The man told you he didn't give Halvorsen a Stradivarius," said Wilson irritably. "Will you forget about the damned Stradivarius?"

"How can I?" I came back. "That's what the case has to be about."

Then Wilson said something that sounded like Yogi Berra. "There isn't one till there is one."

What was that supposed to mean?

"What about the violin in Erik's apartment?" I pushed on. "Is it a Strad?"

Wilson did an eye roll and looked away. Then he looked back at me. "That's all you want, isn't it? To drag some angle into this for a story."

I realized he still hadn't given me an answer. "Erik told us he had one," I argued. "As far as I'm concerned, that fiddle is a Strad until I learn otherwise."

Wilson didn't do an eye roll this time. Or look away, either. He glared at me like somebody in a firing squad taking aim over his rifle sights.

"All right!" He sort of grimaced. "I'll tell you something off-the-record."

Typical. If a cop has something important to tell you, he wants to make sure first that you can't print it.

"I'm not taking anything off the record," I told him, with more bravado than possibly was wise.

"Suit yourself," he tossed out, apparently deciding he was off the hook. "In that case, I will tell you that the violin in question is evidence, and can't be discussed."

A smirk that would have done justice to the Cheshire Cat.

But I had outwitted him. The only thing he could tell me worth keeping off the record was that it *was* a Stradivarius. It was one of those delicious moments when a reporter savors his penetrating analysis.

"Okay," I said with a triumphant smirk of my own.

The thing was, I knew it had to be a Strad. Nothing else made any sense. The only question, as far as I was concerned, was why the killer hadn't taken it. Had he scared himself off by firing those shots? Had he gone to LaPorte to get another one because he had botched the first try? Maybe that was it. Whoever it was was determined to get a Strad somewhere. Whoever it was also knew I was poking around and didn't like it.

I realized these were questions I had better figure out. Because whoever got Erik and LaPorte had given me one of *his* calling cards too. Three of them, in fact.

There wasn't much for me to do at LaPorte's. It would take time for the Assistant Medical Examiner and forensics to do their work. Like Erik's apartment, LaPorte's office was in a shambles, papers strewn all over, drawers open. The killer had been looking for something.

Wilson was willing to say that LaPorte had been shot to death, but that's about all. How many shots and what type of weapon was used had to wait the results of the Medical Examiner's office and ballistics.

Anything else I wanted to know was up to me to find out. Wilson didn't throw me out, though. He seemed resigned that he couldn't get rid of me. But then, it was only fair. I couldn't get rid of him either.

I looked LaPorte's office over, but nothing occurred to me in my groggy state. After a while, Nickerson came in with a woman, whom I recognized as the secretary who had been typing behind the counter when I was here earlier. She came in wooden-legged, like a sleepwalker. She seemed to be in a trance. The death of another person is always a surprise.

Nickerson walked her into LaPorte's office to identify the body. Then I heard a stifled cry.

I drove back to the *Daily Press* and wrote a story for the

Four Star. Then I went home, collapsed into bed, and let the world take care of itself for a while.

8

NATURALLY, WHEN I crawled into bed, I couldn't sleep. Why is it that when you're absolutely dragged out and so exhausted you're practically trembling you can't sleep? All right, I know why. You have jet lag. You're racing along at Mach Two and you try to come to a complete, abrupt halt, but your mind is zipping along out there ahead of you. Your body's ready to crash, but your mind is at thirty thousand feet.

I reached over to the bedside table and picked up Marcus Aurelius's *Meditations*, which is what I usually do when my head is acting like one of the moons orbiting Jupiter.

"Do things external which happen to you distract you?" was Marcus's question to me. "Give yourself time to learn something new and good," he said, "and cease to be whirled around. He who does not observe the movement of his own mind must of necessity be unhappy."

Thus spake Marcus Aurelius to me. "Cease to be whirled around." Well, he was right, of course. I was whirling around. Marcus retired to the bedside table and immediately went to sleep. I did not. I knew what was happening. The damned Erik Halvorsen murder was at the controls of Boeing Fitzgerald, and it was racing along somewhere over Ireland. I obediently attempted, as Marcus had suggested, to "observe the movements" of my own mind.

The "something new and good" that I wanted to learn, of course, was who had attempted to send me to join Hadrian and Augustus and Erik Halvorsen. Because when those parking garage windows exploded behind my head, I realized Wilson was right: this wasn't just a story, it was a homicide investigation. And unless I wanted to be a homicide exhibit, past tense, I had better figure it out.

It was pretty obvious I'd done something to bring the killer after me. But what? It was certainly wonderful. Here he felt threatened enough to shoot at me, and I didn't even know what the hell I was doing.

Of course, I had given the names of the Mozart String Quartet to the police. Was that it? Was one of those seemingly wimpy string players carrying a gun around in his or her violin case? Which one?

Ariel Ryan? No, of course not.

Mark Cohen? The amiable, pudgy Bugs Bunny? Not likely.

His loud wife? Well...

Ingrid Sohn of the nervous, squinty eyes? I couldn't imagine that either.

Mitch Rogers? He was the last one to see Erik alive that night.

Or how about Charles LaPorte? Well, he had a pretty good alibi now. He was dead.

The only way I could figure out *who* was to figure out *why*. And I hadn't a clue. Or had I? It must have begun with Erik and that damned fiddle. Erik on West 11th Street, getting out of Mitch Rogers's car with his violin.

Okay, here comes Toupee Wilson's mugger. He sees Erik's violin case and translates it into enough money to buy cocaine. The mugger jumps out of a darkened doorway, slugs Erik or sticks a gun in his face, grabs the violin, and runs. That's what my experience tells me would have happened. But it didn't.

Okay, strike that. Here's the mugger again. He sees Erik, but he doesn't jump him. Instead, he follows him inside, sneaks up four flights of stairs behind him, and ... what?

I sat up and lighted a Tiparillo. Wouldn't Erik have noticed somebody following him up four flights of stairs on that narrow corner staircase? I was still being whirled around.

Okay. Maybe the mugger is inside the building, waiting for Erik—maybe at the top of the stairs. As Erik opens his apartment door, the mugger steps out of the shadows with a gun. He threatens Erik, takes the fiddle, and scrams down the stairs.

So why didn't he do that? If Erik fought him, the guy could have shot him right there in the hallway.

I got up and walked out into the living room and stared out the window, down into the street, my Tiparillo glowing. The mugger was acting in ways unfamiliar to my police-reporter experience. He could have taken the violin on the street, in the lobby, on the stairs, at Erik's door. But he didn't.

The mugger goes into Erik's apartment. Was he already inside, waiting? Or did Erik let him in, meaning that he knew him? Or did he force Erik inside at gunpoint?

For whatever reason, our mugger didn't take the violin Erik was carrying on the street. Instead, he gets inside the apartment. Why?

I put on a cup of tea and sat at the little kitchen table drinking it, knowing now I would be lucky to sleep at all. My Tiparillo glowed, went out, and was replaced with another.

I was not whirling around so much anymore. The mugger spun off into infinity. In his place, there was somebody else. This was no street mugger. Somebody had to have been inside the apartment. Exit mugger, enter burglar.

All right. Erik comes in and finds a burglar ransacking his apartment. He has turned the place literally upside down, searching for money, silverware, anything. Erik comes in and surprises the burglar, who opens fire and shoots him six times. The guy is so rattled by what he's done that he beats it with nothing.

So here we have a burglar who is cool enough to climb into an apartment and methodically, if not too neatly, ransack the place. He has taken the precaution of arming himself with a gun. He ransacks the apartment either before or after he kills Erik.

If he does it before Erik comes home and finds something to steal, then he's out the window the moment he hears somebody coming. Is it possible he could be panicky enough to kill Erik with six shots and then stick around to ransack the place? Not likely. He must have entered, ransacked the place, found nothing valuable enough to satisfy him, and then been surprised by Erik coming in.

Okay, Erik walks in. He crosses into the dining room and puts his fiddle on the table. He and the burglar see each other. The burglar opens fire. Then he beats it, without bothering to pick up the fiddle, which was right in front of him and easy to carry.

I didn't like the burglar, either. He was too cool and too panicky at the same time. The burglar followed the mugger into the void.

A third presence looms up in Erik's living room.

This somebody has come to Erik Halvorsen's apartment with a gun, and from the way he used it he wasn't somebody used to handling guns. An amateur, all right, as Toupee Wilson had said.

There they stood in Erik's living room, the nervous amateur with a gun and Erik, who had something the killer wanted but that Erik didn't want to give up.

Could it have been somebody from the Algonquin bar that night? Who? Ariel was with me. Marc Cohen? Mitch Rogers? Ingrid Sohn? Somebody else at the table? They all knew Erik had a Stradivarius—or said he did—and a lot of cash. But they took nothing. That would seem to eliminate them all, unless Wilson was right and whoever it was had been scared off.

So what Marcus Aurelius and I had was (one) somebody who followed Erik Halvorsen home, shot him six times, stayed around to ransack the apartment, and left with nothing; or (two) somebody who ransacked Erik Halvorsen's apartment and then, when Erik came in, shot him six times. And left without picking up his violin.

I asked Marcus what he thought, but he was still asleep between his covers on the bedside table.

And I was still being whirled around.

I felt like grabbing Marcus Aurelius and ripping him to shreds. Let him examine the movements of his own mind, if he were so damned wise!

9

BESIDE THE AZURE pool in the shadow of the minaret, wispy lyrics floated into my bedazzled consciousness. "Pale hands I loved, beside the Shalimar..." I was in the Arabian harem of King Shahriyar, listening to Scheherazade beguiling the caliph with tales of jinnis and wazirs and mendicants and Sinbad. Oddly enough, Scheherazade had the bluest of eyes and hair tumbling like a blond waterfall and she accompanied her tale by playing Mozart on a violin. Except that a jinni snuck in and grabbed her fiddle and flew out the window on a magic carpet, and Scheherazade lost the thread of her story, and King Shahriyar called for the wazir to cut off her head—and mine too. Then a great roc flew in the window and I jumped on its back. Off we soared after the jinni on the flying carpet. The great roc looked around at me with red eyes and squawked, "If I catch the jinni for you, I get Scheherazade."

"No way," I yelled, and the roc shook me off his feathery back. I fell through eons of space and time and saw the ground whirling up at me... *whump!*

Amazingly enough, the great red-eyed roc had dropped me through the roof of my apartment building on East 82nd Street, and I woke up in bed.

Well, there it was. The damned case was chasing me in and out of my dreams and in and out of the Arabian Nights.

I checked in with the city desk to tell them I was going to LaPorte's and then drove across town to Columbus Circle.

I parked in the NYP zone and walked down to Carnegie Hall and the violin dealer's.

The place was under siege. It looked like a run on a bank. People were lined up in the corridor outside his office, and, when I shoved my way through, there was Detective Nickerson sitting at the desk inside with Wilma Manning, LaPorte's secretary.

"What's going on?" I asked Nickerson.

He gave me a look of exasperation.

What was going on, I discovered, was that the owners of instruments were there to collect their prized possessions. They had either read my story or heard through the grapevine of musicians that LaPorte had been murdered.

Farther inside, behind the counter, Wilson was talking to a dark-haired man wearing a blue striped apron. I went over.

"How's it going?" I opened.

Wilson gave me an annoyed look. "Peachy."

"Anything turn up?" I went on.

"Yes. Everything," he said with a bit of a smirk.

"What do you mean?"

Wilson introduced me to the blue-striped apron: Otto Becker. He was the luthier behind LaPorte, Wilson explained. Otto Becker smiled.

"Mr. Becker is the chief craftsman here," Wilson said. "He works on all the Stradivari violins. Right, Mr. Becker?"

"Absolutely."

"No one else touches them?" he asked.

"Absolutely not." Becker nodded his head abruptly.

Becker was the head of LaPorte's three-man team of craftsmen. Together they repaired violins—replaced shoulders, took them apart, glued them, filled in nicks—and occasionally made new ones.

"There's a Stradivari missing, right?" I said to Becker.

He didn't hesitate. "Absolutely not."

Wilson smiled.

"Not?"

"There were four Stradivaris here," said Becker. "They are all accounted for.'"

A mutter escaped me. "Impossible."

"What's impossible is you," snapped Wilson. "I'm a detective. I work from facts to the solution. You've already got the solution. Now all you've got to do is twist the facts to fit it. I guess that's what sells papers."

He gazed at me smugly, and I could imagine another Yogi Berrism behind the look: "Nothing's missing until it's missing."

I was still turning the missing nonmissing violin over in my mind when up walked a trim, three-piece suit with styled blond hair.

"Mr. Becker, you've got the Lamberti, for God's sake?" he bubbled anxiously.

"Yes, yes, Mr. Lambert. Of course."

A great sigh escaped from the three-piece suit. "I was going to sue. Oh, yes, I was."

The trim gentleman had to say that, apparently, because he had been rehearsing it in his mind right up to that moment. Just because the violin wasn't missing was no reason to give up his moment.

Becker turned and went to an iron gate that closed off a room behind the counter. He took out a key, opened the door, and disappeared inside the room.

"Name?" Wilson asked the blond.

"Jason Lambert." His eyes darted about. "What happened?"

"That needn't concern you," said old Closed-mouth. He was going down a list.

"Lambert . . . here." He made a mark. "You have a receipt?"

"Yes, of course." Jason Lambert got out a Dunhill wallet and dug out a slip of paper. Wilson took it.

Becker came back out carrying a violin, which he handled

as though it were a vase from the Ming Dynasty. He laid it gently on the glass counter.

"There it is," breathed Lambert.

I glanced curiously at it. An orange shiny surface with a black head. It was gorgeous, all right, but I couldn't tell it from any other violin. Apparently Becker could, though.

"Please pay Mrs. Manning," said Becker.

"What was done to it?" asked Jason Lambert.

"It's all on the bill," said Becker.

"All right." Lambert gently placed the Stradivarius into the violin case Becker had brought and hurried away, back to Wilma Manning and Nickerson near the door.

I looked at Wilson, who was still going over his list.

"They've all been claimed?" I asked.

"No. But they're all here," he said.

"Who owns the other ones?"

Wilson frowned, deciding whether to tell me that it didn't concern me. Then I guess he decided the only way to get rid of me was to go over it.

The other three were owned respectively by the New Jersey Symphony, the Juilliard School, and an Israeli soloist currently enjoying a succès d'estime in New York. He had heard from them all, or they had been contacted.

"So where the hell are we?" I asked. He winced again at the "we."

Where *we* were, he explained, was on the scene of another murder in New York, one of many murders in New York.

"It could be a robbery," he concluded.

"What was taken?"

"I can't go into that."

"Another robbery in which nothing was taken?" I scoffed.

"We don't know that yet."

"Anything from ballistics?"

"Not yet."

So there it was. Another murder in New York that was about nothing. I still couldn't get a Stradivarius into the story, which was the only way to get any real action.

"Why don't you write about the weather?" Wilson suggested.

"Because it wasn't a high wind that blew out those windows behind my head," I told him.

I left.

10

WHEN I GOT back to the office, Ironhead waved me over to the city desk.

"Well?" he demanded, unwrapping a new stogie about the size of the Goodyear blimp.

I could only shrug.

"You don't know who shot at you?" He lighted up and dispersed enough smoke to cover the invasion of Grenada.

"Not the faintest."

"What about the Stradivarius?" he wanted to know.

I sighed. "It didn't come from LaPorte," I said. "But, dammit, there's got to be one in this story."

"I hope so," said Ironhead, "because I don't see much otherwise."

I had to agree, even though it seemed there might be a minor wrinkle there about a *Daily Press* reporter being shot at. Except that nobody but me saw it, and I couldn't link it up to anything.

Still, the recollection of those glass panes exploding kept me going. I got on the phone and called around to every fine violin dealer I could find. No, none of them knew any Erik Halvorsen, and none was missing a Stradivarius.

So I checked out the other three Strads from LaPorte's.

The man at the Juilliard School said yes, they had their violin back, and was I a police officer?

The New Jersey Symphony didn't want to talk at all. "Please check with the police," said a nervous orchestra manager.

The Israeli soloist was in Cleveland, the person who

answered the phone said, but the violin was safe. "There is no reward, sir," he wound up.

I threw aside the phone books and clippings I had used to make my phone calls, sank back in my swivel chair, and lighted a Tiparillo. I leaned back and sought inspiration from the ceiling. Nothing occurred.

And that's when I got my bright idea. Sometimes you have to make a leap in the dark, and I was poised on a cliff over a black void. I couldn't shake the idea that there had to be a Stradivarius. If it didn't come from LaPorte, it came from somewhere else. I had to get a story into the paper that a quarter-million-dollar Stradivarius was missing, and I had thought of how to do it.

It meant calling up Ariel and telling her about the murder of LaPorte, which I had been dreading. She had already read my story and was mildly hysterical.

"Fitz," she wailed, "I can't stand any more of this."

"I know."

"You *don't* know! You just keep plunging along. I've got to get out of here."

"Out of where?"

"New York! It's impossible to live here."

"Where would you go?"

Her words came in a rush. "There are so many places! There's a college in Vermont—Allen State College—that wants a new head of the string department. I've been thinking about it."

I understood what she meant. After you live in New York for a while, you realize what a never-ending hassle it is. You always have the idea in the back of your head that it could be so much easier in Vermont, or somewhere. And after the Big Apple, anything else would be a pushover.

People who live in Manhattan too long sometimes experience a kind of concrete claustrophobia. It's as though you're digging a hole, but with the object of finishing it and getting out. But the deeper you dig, the farther away you get from the light and escape. Then you realize the hole you're digging is a grave.

You always have an idea in your head that there's another life you're going to lead one of these days. Big Jim Lawler always talked about the boat he was going to buy and the life he would lead fishing off Montauk Point. There were other lives in me, too. How long a run can you expect as a cop or a street reporter in New York?

Reporting is a young man's game; when you pass thirty you begin to think of other places, other lives. You begin to think of Ariel and Vermont.

A line drifted into my head from the Ben Hecht–Charles MacArthur newspaper play *The Front Page*, when Hildy Johnson tells the Criminal Court pressroom gang in Chicago why he's leaving while he still can. "You'll all end up on the copy desk—gray-headed, hump-backed slobs, dodging garnishees when you're ninety."

"Do you ever think of leaving?" Ariel asked.

"Sure. Plenty of times."

"Fitz, let's go. Let's get out."

I didn't know what to say. "Let's talk about it, Ariel," I finally said. "I've got to clear up this damned thing first, in any case."

"But why?"

I almost blurted out why—because the killer had me on his list too.

"I just have to."

"Will you think about it? Vermont?"

I told her I would. Then I asked her for the phone numbers of everyone who had been at the Algonquin bar that night.

"What for?" she asked.

"I want to be able to quote them that they heard Erik say he had a Stradivarius. And that he showed it to them."

Well, I was loony if I thought any of them would talk to me after I had sicked the cops on them, she informed me.

"They'll talk to me," I told her.

"What makes you think so?"

"Because people in a murder case can't resist talking to a reporter."

I was right about that. When I got Mark Cohen on the phone in Teaneck, New Jersey, I couldn't stop him and his large wife Sylvia from coming over the line at me like shaving cream.

They had read my story, too. At least I had developed a tight little knot of faithful readers. The whole thing was a scandal, they told me, especially the murder of Hally, because who was going to act as manager for the Mozart String Quartet now? Who was going to pay Mark?

"Have you checked out Ariel?" shrieked Sylvia, who apparently was on an extension. "No, of course not! All you see is her phony good looks!"

I was going to ask what was phony about them, but Sylvia was just getting warmed up.

"Hally dumped her for Ingrid. Did you know that? No, of course not. Men are all such fools. She had a perfect motive."

"What motive?"

"Ingrid!"

For that matter, Sylvia went on, had anybody checked out Ingrid? "That little cookie is totally manipulative and a card-carrying bitch."

Then Mark spoke up to say the investigation should center on Mitch Rogers because he was known to be "the most dishonest man in the history of Local Eight-oh-two."

"Why is that?" I asked.

"Because everyone hates him. Ask Sylvia."

I didn't have to ask Sylvia, because she yelled into the extension. "He's right. Set that totally in stone! Why didn't he hire Mark for 'The Phantom of the Opera'? Are you trying to tell me Mark isn't the best free-lance cellist in New York City?"

I wouldn't dream of it.

Oh, the whole thing was transparent, Mark said on the other line. "How do you think Mitch drives a Mercedes? By winning the Lottery? Let's face it, all contractors are thieves."

"Are you including Hally?" I asked.

"Hally? Don't make me laugh. He'd hardly got started, and already he was the biggest goniff in town."

I had felt they would talk, but it was difficult dealing with twin Niagaras. I asked if there was any other reason to suspect Mitch Rogers.

Niagara Number One, the shrill one, blasted into my ear. "I told you, Ingrid!"

"What about her?"

"For a reporter, you don't listen, you know that? I would have thought you were trained to listen. Now, *listen*. Ingrid dumped Mitch and grabbed Hally when Hally dumped Ariel because Ariel thinks she's the reincarnation of Grace Kelly on toast."

"I see," I managed. Enlightening.

"Mitch was always trying to get Ingrid back, although why is a mystery best left to the imagination. The man has a wife and children, and he goes after Ingrid Sohn. Figure that one—"

"Wait a minute," I interrupted. "Are you saying Ingrid got Hally, or Mitch?"

"I wouldn't trust either one of them," she declared flatly.

Terrific.

After the Cohens had run down a little, I got around to asking about the violin, which was the purpose of the call. Did they know whether Hally really had a Stradivarius?

"He said he did," Mark agreed. "I heard him."

"And somebody killed him, didn't they?" added Sylvia. "And Mitch was the last one with him."

"You think Mitch would kill Hally for a violin?" I asked.

"I think he'd kill him for a shoulder pad."

"Set that in stone."

Then Cohen said if I were going to say anything rotten—"even though it's true"—about Mitch Rogers, would I please not use his name. "I mean, I have to work with the goddam creep."

I told them thanks for their help and began to wonder if classical musicians were all that disciplined and controlled after all.

I called Ingrid Sohn next but got no answer. So I tried the most dishonest man in the history of Local 802.

"My God, why did you drag me into this?" wailed Mitch Rogers.

"Sorry. You were the last one to see him that night."

"My God!" he howled. "Just because we had an argument, everybody wants to pin it on me!"

"What argument?"

"It was nothing," he protested. "Just sitting in the car."

"About Ingrid?"

"Who told you that?"

"I just heard it."

Mitch Rogers muttered under his breath. "Fiddle players . . . they're all children."

"I'm interested in the violin Hally had," I told him. "Was it a Stradivarius? He said it was."

"Jesus, I don't know," he protested. "The guy was a wheeler-dealer, or he thought he was."

"You looked at it," I told him. "Seemed pretty interested in it."

"Well, sure," Rogers came back. "Who wouldn't be?"

"You drove Ingrid and Hally home?"

"Yes. Ingrid and I did."

"I thought you dropped Ingrid off first and then took Hally home alone."

There was a pause. "Oh. Yes. Isn't that what I said?"

"No."

69

"Look, I dropped off Ingrid, then took Hally down to the Village. He got out, and that was that."

"You still didn't tell me what you quarreled about."

"It was nothing. Does it matter?"

"Everything matters in a murder case, Mitch."

"All right. About Ingrid. He was trying to make a move on her. Trying to play Fritz Kreisler. I told him he was Turkey-in-the-Straw and to leave her alone."

I was getting dizzy trying to figure out the musical chairs.

"Did anybody throw any punches?"

"What? Two fiddle players? What are you, insane? We might have tried to kick each other in the crotch if we hadn't been inside the car. But no hands, for God's sake."

He was pretty wound up, all right.

"You're not going to write about this, are you?" he finally asked me.

It always amazes me when somebody talks to a reporter and then wonders if he's going to write something.

"All I'm interested in is whether you heard Hally say he had a Stradivarius," I said, dodging his direct question.

"Sure. We all heard that. Didn't you?"

I had heard it, all right. And now I had Mitch and the two Cohens willing to say they had heard it too.

11

PEOPLE LIKE STORIES about criminals who are either very smart or very stupid. So I wrote a story about the murder of LaPorte and tacked on a shirttail about the murder of Erik Halvorsen. Since they were both violin stories, I could link them up.

Then I stuck in that Erik had told everyone he had a Stradivari, but the ignorant killer hadn't even bothered to pick up a quarter-million dollar instrument. So there it sat in the Police Department property clerk's office.

It got a little better play than the original story about Erik's murder; it went on page four, as I had hoped.

Even Ironhead was pleased.

"All right," he bubbled, letting out a cascade of roiling smoke. "Not a bad yarn."

Then he caught himself. It's bad form to tell any reporter that any story is worth a tinker's damn.

"You should have got this in the first story," he finished.

Then I waited for somebody to get in touch with me. Maybe somebody who wanted to buy the Stradivarius from Erik. Maybe the killer himself would get rattled. You never know.

Well, it worked faster than I could have hoped. The three-star had barely hit the streets when I got a call at Costello's, where Glenn the switchboard guy tracked me down.

Only the call wasn't from a tipster or from somebody who would break the case and win me a Pulitzer. No, the call was from a screaming raving smoldering angry Detective Wilson, as I discovered when I returned the call and got the West 10th Street squad in the Village.

"Where did you get that load of crap?" he wanted to know.

"Which load of crap in particular?"

"That business about a Stradivarius!"

Calmly, I explained the obvious to the thick-headed dick. "Wilson, I told you Erik said it was a Strad."

A confiscated bomb going off at the Rodman's Neck bomb disposal site in the Bronx wouldn't have made more noise. Wilson let me know that I was five kinds of a lunkhead, a clown, and a dope, among other things.

"Goddammit, the boss is on my neck and we're going to have every music nut in the city calling up here," he howled. I realized what was going on, all right. My story about a Stradivarius would kick up interest and make more work for him. Too bad.

"Look, Wilson," I said, "a dumb killer missing a Strad is a good story. I can't help it."

"Oh, you can't, huh?" Sarcasm poured from him like Aunt Jemima syrup. "Well, did it ever occur to you to check your facts before you print them? Or is that against the code of screw-ups?"

"What facts?"

"Goddammit, it isn't a Stradivarius!"

Silence benumbed me.

"What?" I finally got out. "But—"

"But what?"

"We saw it . . . in Halvorsen's apartment."

"We saw a *violin*, not a Stradivarius!"

I felt I was falling from the feathered back of the giant roc again.

"It wasn't?"

"No!"

"But Erik told us—"

"Erik told us, Erik told us!" Wilson was fuming. "Well,

I checked it out, and it's just an ordinary damned fiddle! Now, I want a retraction printed, goddammit! There is no Stradivarius in this case, and I'm not going to be forced to spend time on a damned bungled mugging."

Now I'm the one who exploded. "Why in the hell didn't you tell me?" I shouted. "How the hell are we going to work together if you keep me in the dark all the time?"

He seemed to be strangling.

"If I'm on the story—" I started again, but got no further.

"I don't want you on this story!"

"Tough titty!"

"I want a retraction," he said stubbornly. "The violin in his apartment was not a Stradivarius, and there is no proven link to Charles LaPorte!"

I was gripping the phone in a stranglehold and red sparks spun in my head. What had happened to that delicious moment of penetrating analysis when I had concluded that the violin had to be a Strad? The damned sly dick had tricked me. He was going to tell me off the record something as simpy as that the violin was *not* a Strad?

I tried to think, but the red sparks were engulfing me. "I don't get it," I finally blurted out. "It had to be a Strad. It doesn't make sense otherwise."

"You mean it doesn't make a crappy story!"

Still I couldn't let go. What the hell could have happened?

"Wait a minute." It dawned on me. "He must have pulled a switch."

"Who?"

"The killer! He took the Strad and left another violin in its place."

"Is that so?" Aunt Jemima syrup flowed through the phone. I felt I was about to be inundated with warm goo.

"Sure! And he left it in plain sight, so—"

"Huh!" A lump of sarcasm in the goo.

But I felt I had it now. "That's it, Wilson! Will you stop

being such a horse's patoot? Did you dust it for prints? The killer's fingerprints must be all over it if he's the bumbling amateur you say he is."

"Oh, there's a bumbling amateur here, all right," he spat, "but it's not the killer." I was supremely disinterested in the identity of the bumbler he obviously had in mind.

"Were there prints on the violin, or is this another state secret?" I demanded.

Then came the threatened syrup. "Oh, there were prints on it."

"OK!"

"Erik Halvorsen's prints."

"Erik's?"

"That's right. A violinist puts prints on his violin every time he plays it. Thumb prints. Palm prints. Index fingerprints. Every goddam print anybody could want. All his."

I was a waffle, ready to be devoured.

"Nobody else's?" the waffle asked plaintively.

"No. Believe me, I tried to find yours."

"OK, so he wore gloves," I suggested hopefully.

"Gloves, huh? Well, maybe that's it. The killer came there with a violin and put it in Halvorsen's violin case. Oddly enough, it was Erik's own instrument."

"It was Erik's?"

"That's right. His very own. A Guadagnini he purchased for eight thousand bucks in 1978, for which I have the receipt."

"Jupiter Optimus Maximus."

"Which brings us back to square one," said Wilson. "There is *no* Stradivarius in this case!"

"Listen, Wilson, I reported a fact. Erik said it was a Strad, and that's what I reported."

"Well, now we know that what he said wasn't true. So now you can print *that*!"

"Politicians say things all the time that aren't true, and

there aren't enough columns in the whole damned sheet to straighten them out," I spluttered idiotically.

"I'm calling your city desk," he snapped then, getting calmer and considerably more vicious. "I get a retraction, and I don't see your dopey puss anymore, or I call your city desk."

Whump. Errrrrrr.

Pompous dick! Who the hell did he think he was talking to? Did he think he could scare a *Daily Press* reporter? The idea was ludicrous.

I stomped back to the bar and sipped my mug of beer and went through thirty-five variations on what I would do to him. I lighted a Tiparillo and bathed myself in enjoyment over what Ironhead would say when he heard some dumb dick trying to intimidate us.

Let him call Ironhead and say . . . and say what?

Wilson's voice floated into my head. "There's no goddam Stradivarius in this case!"

Then I heard Ironhead's disembodied voice. "No Stradivarius? Are you telling me one of my reporters is so stupid as to write about a nonexistent fiddle?"

Wilson again. "That's exactly what I'm telling you."

My enjoyment of Wilson skewered over a fire began to lessen. Maybe Ironhead wouldn't tell him off strongly enough. Maybe Ironhead would even listen.

I gulped my mug of beer.

Suddenly, I realized the skewer was not stuck through Wilson at all but through someone I knew intimately. What if Ironhead found out I'd made a minor mistake? Such as writing a story about something that existed only in my inflamed brain?

Mild concern slid through me, followed by fear, fright, and then panic.

Then I realized there was nothing to worry about after all. I could easily fix things. Wilson had told me how, and he wasn't being totally unreasonable. All I had to do was tell Ironhead I wanted to print a retraction.

A *retraction!*

A vision roiled up in my mind of Krakatau, the great volcano between Java and Sumatra in Indonesia that erupted in 1883 and wiped out an island and all its inhabitants.

A retraction? Reporters who told Ironhead they had to print retractions usually found themselves also retracted, covering Brooklyn police on the lobster shift.

Misery invaded every nook and cranny of my worthless being. I was dead meat.

Why hadn't I listened to Ariel? She told me Erik didn't really have a Strad and was only blowing smoke up everybody's grumper. But no, I had to have a Stradivarius, because otherwise it was just a wasted killing about nothing, as Wilson had tried to tell me. The damned know-it-all.

And now I was faced with telling Ironhead I had to print a retraction. I wondered if there were any tramp freighters leaving soon from Bush Terminal in Brooklyn.

12

I WISH I could tell you I faced up to my problem and told Ironhead we had to print a retraction. I wish I could tell you I admitted to Wilson that he was right. I wish I could tell you I did anything at all.

But I didn't. What I did was go looking for that hole I had been digging so I could climb down into it out of sight.

I had succeeded better than I knew in getting Ironhead's interest. Because now that I had a Strad in the story, he wanted a follow.

"Anything more on that fiddle?" he asked me.

"I don't know," I hedged.

"What?" His eager face went into arrest. "You've been bugging me about it, and now you don't know?"

"I'm checking. But it may be petering out," I stalled.

"Goddammit." Ironhead flared up, "Call up that dumb dick and bust his butt."

I couldn't even respond to that, because the last person I wanted to call up, or ever hear from again, was Detective Toupee Wilson.

"You want me to call him?" Ironhead offered in an unusual outburst of assistance.

Good God!

"No, no," I mumbled. "I'm working on it." I gave him a hopeful look. "Unless you've got something else for me?"

"What?"

I slipped away from the city desk. Like a craven rodent, I decided simply to drop the whole damned thing. What else could I do?

In the first place, I couldn't face Ironhead and tell him I had foully besmirched the pages of the *Daily Press*—*his Daily Press*. In the second place, I didn't see how I could do anything when Wilson wouldn't talk to me. And in the third place, which was probably the first place, I couldn't face Ariel and tell her I was dropping the whole thing.

Such situations cause a reporter to wind up sitting at the end of the bar in Costello's pondering the vicissitudes of fate. I even avoided Ariel, which took a lot of vicissitude, and began to wonder wistfully if we could both simply slip out of town in the dead of night.

After a few days I had almost convinced myself that the whole mess had blown over. But a letter eventually reaches you even from China. The Chinese mailman loomed up in the person of Glenn the switchboard guy, who asked me why I didn't seem to care about all my phone messages.

"What messages?"

Glenn explained he couldn't go running around nagging everybody about their calls. He was only one person, and people had to come and check the message file.

"This broad keeps calling."

"What broad?"

Glenn riffled phone message slips. "Ariel Ryan."

The face and form leaped into my receptive mind.

"What's the message?"

"That's it."

Wonderful. Switchboard guys at newspapers are not in the habit of taking down long, detailed memos. I assumed it meant I was supposed to call her. I did.

She came on the phone all excited.

"Fitz? I've been calling and calling!"

"Sorry."

"Nobody ever answers over there," she complained. "Isn't anybody there?"

There was no use explaining the haphazard way a newspaper operates. If your phone rings and you aren't there, it might ring forever unnoticed. Or maybe Bike O'Malley will grab it up and snort, "Yeah?" If the person asks for you, Bike might gargle, "S'not here," and hang up. Or Paul Cresskill might snatch it up and, if the party asks to leave a message, will mutter, "Call Western Union." Of course the switchboard is supposed to pick up after three rings, but the switchboard guy might be busy ordering from Classic Pizza or the Grand Central Deli for somebody, or he might be tied up talking to some wacko complaining that the *Daily Press* is a fascist rag, or communist, or socialist, or maybe simply a disgrace.

"I only got the message today," I said lamely.

"Listen, I heard from that man."

"What man?"

"The one who wanted the Stradivarius from Hally."

"What?" I said. "I thought you told me Hally didn't have a Strad."

"I didn't think he did."

I was confused. "But Ariel, the cops looked at Hally's violin, and it's just a regular fiddle."

Ariel was agitated. Whether it was or wasn't, she didn't know. All she knew was that Hally was dead, and that a man had approached her Sunday after the Mozart String Quartet played another concert at St. Randolph's Church on Park Avenue.

"You're still playing . . . without Hally?"

Yes, of course, she told me. "We've got a contract. We *have* to. Laila Vann is subbing."

A man had come up to her afterward and had asked for Erik.

"I'd forgotten that Hally had talked to this man several times earlier. I didn't realize he was the one who wanted the Strad."

"What did he say?"

"He wanted to get in touch with Hally. I didn't know what to say, I was so stunned. So I didn't tell him about . . ."

The man had told her that he needed the violin soon.

"Did you get his name?"

"Yes," she said. "He gave me his card. Fred Cerutti. He's in the Pan Am building." She gave me a phone number.

"Who is he?"

"I don't know. I remember now he used to come to the concerts, and he always talked with Hally afterward. But he's the one. Does that help?"

"Does that help what?"

"Help you find who killed Hally!"

I stared at the phone in my hand as though it were a live snake. I wanted to drop it before it bit me. I wanted to tell her I had to drop the Halvorsen murder, because it was leading me inexorably toward Ironhead's doghouse and Toupee Wilson's wrath. I wanted to tell her that Wilson wouldn't give me the time of day if he were standing under the big clock in Grand Central Terminal, and that I already faced the to-be-avoided-at-all-costs problem of asking Ironhead to print a retraction for even mentioning the damned Stradivarius.

But what I said was, "I guess so."

"You *guess* so?" Irritation. "I get the information you wanted, and you *guess* so?"

A sigh slid out of me. This kind of thing happens to reporters all the time. Or at least it happens to me. People assume you're panting to cover their story and can go out on anything you wish.

Of course, in this case I was panting for Ariel, but I was afraid that if I chased this story any further Ironhead would be panting for me. And not with love, either. If I left the story alone, I was probably safe from Wilson and Ironhead, but Ariel would be unhappy. Wonderful.

"What else does it say on the card?" I asked her.

"Uh, it says 'oil.' "

Figured. An oil man. He could afford a Strad. So I called the number on Fred Cerutti's card.

"Cerutti. Home or business?"

"What?"

"Do you want oil for a residence or a business?" asked the woman on the phone.

"I want Mr. Cerutti."

The phone flipped over and music came blasting into my ear. I can't stand these places where they put you on hold and then zonk you with blaring, howling sound. I always want to yell "Shut up!" at the music, but Placido Domingo or whoever it was had no interest in listening to me but went on emotionally about Aida or somebody. Because what was coming over the phone was opera. It's not that I don't like opera, as long as I can get it on a record without going to the Met, but I don't want it in the middle of a phone call.

"Cerutti!" Another assistant.

"Fitzgerald, *Daily Press*, here."

"Oh! Well, hello!"

"Mr. Cerutti, please."

"You got 'im."

So it wasn't an assistant but the inner sanctum of the petroleum tycoon himself. I had this picture of J. Paul Getty in a mammoth carpeted office in the Pan Am building.

"Mr. Cerutti, I'm calling about Erik Halvorsen."

"Yeah, sure!" His voice rose in interest. "I'm glad you called. I gotta get going on this thing."

"Pardon me?" I said.

"I haven't heard from him. He was supposed to bring the Strad, and then I didn't hear any more."

The portrait of J. Paul Getty smeared into something a little more rough cut.

"When did you talk to him last?" I asked.

"Let's see . . . a week ago Sunday, was it? Yeah, Sunday."

J. Paul Getty became an oilfield wildcatter, maybe even wearing cowboy boots. Hand-tooled ones, of course.

Sunday, I thought. Erik was killed Sunday night.

81

"Did Erik show you the Stradivarius, Mr. Cerutti?"

"Sure."

"You saw it?"

"Yeah, sure, I saw it. Why?"

"Could I come around and talk to you?" I suggested.

"Yeah, sure," he said. "Come on. Erik told me you wanted the story."

I wasn't sure I had heard him correctly. "Erik said *I* wanted to do a story?"

"*Daily Press*, right? It's OK. I'm willing to let you have it."

"Uh-huh," I grunted, not sure of what else to say.

"The only thing is, though," he went on, "it's got to run with Veronica's picture. So you'll have to wait till I give it to her, and then you can get your picture."

I was puffing on a Tiparillo, trying to take it all in.

"Erik told you this?"

"I told him OK," said Cerutti. "So what's it gonna be, center spread or front page?"

"What?"

"Veronica's picture."

I bit off the end of my Tiparillo. "Erik told you Veronica's picture would be on the front page of the *Daily Press*?"

"Sure. That's why I decided to buy from him."

13

YOU KNOW HOW it is when you get an idea in your mind to solve a problem, and you don't realize that it might create an even bigger one? The one thing in the world I couldn't face was asking Ironhead about that retraction. I would rather arm-wrestle a polar bear. And here was a way out. Fred Cerutti, oil tycoon, was telling me there *was* a Stradivarius and he had seen it.

All I had to do was prove I hadn't made up that violin, and Ironhead would not be in a position to degrade and humiliate and retract me.

All right, I admit I found it wrenching to disappoint Ariel. Talking to her again had set Tannhäuser playing inside my head. I also was intrigued by Cerutti's words and thought everything could come out all right if I could bring back a good story to Ironhead.

I should have realized that nothing ever comes out all right when you're dealing with someone composed of equal parts of Genghis Khan and Mad King Ludwig.

Anyway, I told Cerutti I'd like to come over and talk to him, and he said come on. I said I would walk over right now.

"Walk?" He sounded surprised.

"Yeah. You're in the Pan Am building? We're just down the street."

He laughed. "Oh. Naw, that's just the office. I'm in Queens, off Metropolitan Avenue."

I walked down to the NYP parking zone on 40th Street, coaxed my asthmatic Monte Carlo to life, and drove through the Queens Midtown Tunnel and out along the Long Island Expressway. You get off at Woodhaven Boulevard, go up through Rego Park past St. John's Cemetery where they bury the mobsters, and to Metropolitan Avenue in a neighborhood called Glendale.

Driving along looking for Cerutti's place, I kept trying to figure out what in the world Erik Halvorsen had told him. Apparently Fred Cerutti thought he had a very big story that anybody would do anything to get. Well, of course, buying a $250,000 fiddle for your girlfriend might be pretty monumental to you, but it will not necessarily mean the front page or even the center spread. And no reporter is crazy enough to promise anybody a story will be in the paper, even on the back pages. But then, Erik had not been a reporter but a huckster trying to sell a very expensive instrument. He apparently had made good use of my *Daily Press* business card.

Just past Metropolitan Avenue there's a bridge leading to Forest Park, and the Long Island Rail Road runs under it. Off on a side street I found Cerutti's, an immense grimy yard full of lumbering silver oil trucks all emblazoned with CERUTTI in big green letters; and in a grimy office around the back I found Frederick Cerutti himself, a short, dark, intense man in a well-cut suit and a pencil mustache.

"Mr. Cerutti?" I asked, stepping in.

"Hey! *Daily Press*!"

Fred Cerutti hopped up energetically and came out a little swinging door to shake hands. "Come on," he said, "let's get outa here."

He led me outside to a grimy Lincoln Continental, parked among the oil trucks, and drove out of the yard and then over into Forest Hills, which is the neighborhood next door to Glendale.

Off Queens Boulevard, he parked outside a restaurant on Austin Street and led me inside.

When we were at a table, he ordered drinks and then

leaned across the table at me.

"So what's with the Strad?" he said.

I tried to do a quick study of Fred Cerutti. He certainly was a no-frills man who moved quickly. No J. Paul Getty but a Queens entrepreneur who delivered heating oil to homes and businesses sat across from me talking about buying a violin worth possibly a quarter of a million dollars.

Then he laughed happily. "You're wondering what a guy like Fred Cerutti is doing buying a Stradivarius?" He smiled hugely. "Some kind of story, huh?"

"You bet," I said, wanting to hear more.

"I can't wait to see Veronica's face."

Yes, I wanted to see Veronica too. "Veronica is ... a friend?"

Fred Cerutti's face became serious. "Veronica is my daughter. Didn't Erik tell you?"

"I guess I forgot," I said. "The violin is for your daughter?"

"Sure. You didn't think *I* was gonna play at Carnegie Hall, did you? Sure it's for Veronica. She's gonna go crazy."

I sat back and lighted a Tiparillo.

"Do you read the papers, Mr. Cerutti?"

Cerutti sipped his scotch and water. "Naw, not much. Sports, you know? *Petroleum News*. Got too damned much other stuff to read. You wouldn't believe it. Mostly the *Journal*."

"Journal?"

"*Wall Street Journal*."

He had me there. I never read that.

"Erik is dead."

Cerutti looked at me blankly. It didn't seem to register. "What?"

"It was in the paper."

"Wow," Cerutti mumbled. "I didn't see it. Dead?"

"I think somebody killed him over the violin."

Cerutti seemed stunned into silence. He looked at me and shook his head. Then he spread his arms apart in a gesture of bewilderment.

"Boy!"

"You said you saw the violin?"

Cerutti's left arm went up, as though to say Wait a minute. He cocked his head and glanced at me and put it into words. "Wait a minute, now. This really gets me."

I watched the sturdy oil distributor's face as he shifted gears before my eyes from a relaxed and loving father chatting about his daughter and her music to the wary businessman he had to be to have gotten where he was.

"You're not here about Veronica, are you?" he said. "You're here about murder."

I nodded.

"Huh!" He studied me much the way I had been studying him, giving me a look that would probably knock the price of oil down a few cents a gallon. He leaned across the table and said it with a lot of conviction.

"I don't want you writing about my daughter."

"Well..."

"Is that understood?"

The price of oil fell a few more cents.

"And I don't want my name mentioned."

"Mr. Cerutti, these things can get very tricky."

I tried to explain, but his grimace told me I could never make it in business against men like him.

"OK," I said. "I'll keep your name out of it."

"And Veronica's."

"All right."

"What in the hell happened to Erik?" he wanted to know, peering intently at me across the table. I filled him in on the basic details. He let out a low whistle.

"Now, about the violin," I said. "You say you saw it?"

"Sure, he showed it to me. I had to be sure it was the

real thing, didn't I?"

"And how could you be sure?"

Cerutti told me that he and Erik had gone together to a violin dealer in Manhattan and had showed it to an expert.

"Where in Manhattan?"

"By Carnegie Hall. Leeb ... Van Leeb. I got his name from Veronica's teacher."

"You picked the expert?"

Cerutti gave me a look. "Sure, I picked the expert. You don't think I'd let *him* pick him, do you? I had to be sure."

"And the expert said it was a Stradivarius?" I asked.

"That's right. The genuine article."

"How could he tell?"

Cerutti leaned across the table in the Austin Street bar and smiled. "He looked at it for about two seconds," Cerutti tapped the table with his finger. "Absolutely authentic."

I leaned back and puffed my Tiparillo. Such things were a mystery to me. Two seconds and he was certain?

"How was it left?"

"Mr. Halvorsen was going to draw up the papers and deliver the papers and the violin to me Monday."

"This coming Monday?"

"No. Last Monday. We shook hands on it. But I bought the bow right away."

"The bow?"

"Yeah. The bow."

I hadn't even thought of that. Of course, there would have to be a violin bow.

"Was it a Stradivari, too?"

"Oh, yes. Mr. Van Leeb said it was the real thing."

"How much did you pay him for it?"

Cerutti leaned back away from the table. "Well, it was considerable."

"How'd you pay him ... by check?"

"That's right."

Well. That would account for the extra money Erik seemed to have.

"How much did you agree to pay for the violin?"

"Enough."

So there it was. Fred Cerutti was going to keep his own counsel on the money end.

"Where's the bow now?" I asked him.

"I've got it."

I was a little annoyed at his reserve and considered telling him that Detective Wilson of the psychedelic sport coats just might want to seize it for evidence. But I kept my own counsel too. We would see what we would see.

"Did Erik tell you where he was getting the violin?"

Cerutti frowned thoughtfully. "Well, I assumed it was his."

"Is that what he told you?"

No, Cerutti admitted, Erik hadn't said. Only that he had a Strad to sell.

And that was all Cerutti could tell me. He had gone to Sunday night concerts at St. Randolph's with Veronica and had heard the Mozart String Quartet play. His daughter had been entranced by the group and had sighed that she would love to have a really fine violin.

"I took her up and introduced her to Mr. Halvorsen," he told me. "He let her play his violin. Well, you should have seen the look on Veronica's face when she played that instrument! It was ... angelic! And that's when I decided I'd get her the best violin I could find."

He had taken Erik aside and asked if he could help him find a fine violin. Money was no object. To his surprise, Erik Halvorsen had told him he might have a Strad for sale.

"I was absolutely tickled," he grinned at me. "Imagine ... a Stradivarius! I didn't even think you could buy them."

A magnificent dream had opened up for Fred Cerutti that day. Veronica was an accomplished violinist, his only child, and the dearest thing in his life. He had lost his wife three years ago. In November, Veronica would be playing at Carnegie Hall with the Metropolitan Youth Symphony Orchestra, he told me.

"She's principal second violinist," he said proudly.

Something popped into my head. "Does Veronica know Dennis Hanley?" I asked.

Cerutti looked at me in surprise. "Do you know Dennis?"

"I know his teacher."

Well, of course Veronica knew Dennis, and so did Fred.

"He just beat her out as concertmaster," said Cerutti. "A fine young man. Listen, between you and me, I think she's sweet on him."

And actually, that was another reason he wanted the Stradivari for Veronica. "The next time they compete, she's gonna wipe him out." He smiled. Then his face went glum. "Or at least, she was going to."

After the first concert series ended at St. Randolph's, he said, he talked with Erik several times and was told that Erik was searching for a Stradivarius for him. Then about a month later, the Mozart String Quartet had returned to St. Randolph's for another series of concerts, and that's when Erik had brought the Strad.

"When was this?"

"What, two-three weeks ago?"

"He was playing the Strad at the concerts?"

"Yes. God, it was beautiful!"

After the first concert, Cerutti and Erik had gone to see Van Leeb, Cerutti had been satisfied with what he was getting, and Cerutti had purchased the bow. Then it was a matter of Erik doing the paperwork, getting the certificate of authenticity.

"He was supposed to deliver it on Monday, after the second concert," said Cerutti.

"I was at that concert," I told him.

That had been the night we all went to the Algonquin

and Erik had bragged about the Strad and displayed it for us.

"What happened on Monday?"

"I was at my office in the Pan Am building, but he didn't show up," said Cerutti. "I figured, you know, more damned paperwork."

But when Cerutti went to the next concert, Erik wasn't there. That's when he had approached Ariel Ryan.

So there it was. Erik had been playing the violin under the noses of the Mozart String Quartet, boasting about it, ready to make the biggest deal in his life. Then he had gone home and met . . . who?

We walked out of the restaurant onto Austin Street, and Cerutti stopped for a moment, lost in thought.

"*Were* you going to put Veronica's picture in the paper?" he asked me, rather embarrassed.

I felt this was a man who wanted to hear it the way it is. "I'm sorry, I didn't know anything about it."

He clamped his mouth together. I realized I would not like to be somebody who crossed this compact dynamo. And I realized how Erik had gotten to him through a chink in his armor, the principal second violinist of the Metropolitan Youth Symphony Orchestra.

14

CERUTTI DROVE ME back to my car, and I headed back into Manhattan on Queens Boulevard, my mind swirling with more questions than ever. The biggest one, of course, was who had known about the violin and had been waiting for Erik at home. The second biggest one was where he had gotten the Stradivarius to begin with and how he could have been carrying it around like that.

I drove the grumbling Monte Carlo along Queens Boulevard past more cemeteries, through Sunnyside, and across the 59th Street Bridge into Manhattan. Then a zig down Second Avenue to 57th Street, and a zag across 57th to the West Side. I parked in the NYP zone at Columbus Circle and walked down to Carnegie Hall, its old yellow-brick sides rigged with scaffolding as it underwent some kind of renovation.

A couple of doors past the Russian Tea Room I found the address and rode up in the elevator. Inside, there was a huge room two stories high, and in a maroon-carpeted office containing a large safe with a bust of Beethoven on top I found Hendrik Van Leeb.

I don't know what I had expected: probably a wizened, colorful-looking character out of Dresden wearing wire-rimmed glasses and speaking like Count Bismarck. What came striding out of his office after a secretary summoned him was a tall, rangy, imposing gentleman with dark hair and the manner and appearance of a theatrical producer. Not a Walt Disney Gepetto but a self-assured impresario walked up to me.

"Yes?" he said expectantly.

"Ed Fitzgerald, *Daily Press*."

Van Leeb's eyes quickened with interest. "Ah, yes, you called me about a Stradivarius."

"I did?"

"Didn't you?"

Then I remembered he was one of the dealers I had checked out.

"I'm still looking," I told him.

"Ah." He smiled. "Aren't we all?"

"The first thing I want to tell you is that I don't know what I'm talking about."

Van Leeb smiled broadly. "Well, few people do, but not many admit it."

"I'm told you can look at a violin and tell in two seconds if it's a Stradivarius."

"That is true."

"How can you tell?"

Van Leeb walked me back into his office, gestured for me to sit, and then went behind his desk, which looked like something out of Napoleon's study.

"Well, of course," he said as we sat down, "years of experience. The family business goes back to Mittenwald. I grew up dealing in fine violins, and there's nothing that looks like a Stradivarius. There's an orange-yellow varnish that no one has ever succeeded in duplicating—or even analyzing. There's a look, a craftsmanship. Unique, don't you see?"

"How many are there still around?"

Van Leeb pondered a moment. "Seven hundred . . . eight, maybe. That's violins, violas, and cellos, you understand."

"Is that all you would do, look at it?"

No, no, said Van Leeb. The look would tell the story, all right. But then he would check the papers.

"What papers?"

"Documentation. Previous owners. The certificate."

I took out a blue box of Tiparillos and looked at him.

"Mind?"

"Go right ahead."

I lighted the Tiparillo and puffed on it. So, a Stradivarius had a set of papers, a pedigree, like a racehorse or a royal duke.

"You mean every Stradivarius has a set of documents?"

He nodded slowly. "Usually. Every once in a century, a lost one turns up without papers. But that's very rare. People walk in to see me carrying a fiddle they found in the attic, followed by three lawyers, each one unwilling to trust the other. I take one look and say no."

"Do you remember somebody bringing in a Stradivarius a couple of weeks ago and asking your opinion? A violinist named Erik Halvorsen?"

Van Leeb's eyes lighted up. "Ah, yes! I remember the violin distinctly. But he didn't give me his name."

"Was it a Strad?"

"Oh, yes. I was not allowed to examine it long enough to tell you which one, but it was authentic, I can tell you that."

"What would you say it was worth?"

"Ahhh." He thought that one over. "Maybe three hundred thousand dollars."

I let out smoke.

"Maybe more. That's the one you're looking for?"

I nodded.

"May I ask why?" His eyes were zeroed in on me now.

"I think somebody was murdered because of it."

Van Leeb nodded somberly, apparently not overly surprised.

"Yes, some of them have rather bloody histories."

"So if you were selling one, you would have to have the documentation?"

"Oh, yes. Then, when you know which one it is, you can examine the photographs to make sure it's what it purports to be: the Duke of Edinburgh or the Empress Catherine or whatever."

"What's that?" I asked, confused.

"What's what?"

"The Duke of Edinburgh?"

"The name of the violin."

"They have *names?*"

Van Leeb chuckled. "Yes. Usually a Stradivarius is known by the name of its most famous owner. So, I would check the *Iconography*."

I was at sea as Hendrik Van Leeb talked. But eventually he told me that there is a comprehensive list of every known Stradivari instrument, complete with photographs, called *The Violin Iconography of Antonio Stradivari*, which I would find at the Lincoln Center Library if I were interested.

"If it's a Stradivarius, it will be listed."

"But I have to have the name of it?"

"Ah, yes."

And then something popped into my head. Somebody had asked for a Stradivarius by name at LaPorte's.

"Did you ever hear of a Strad called the Lamberti?" I asked.

"The Lamberti?" Van Leeb mused. "I think so. Gilberto Lamberti."

"Who's Gilberto Lamberti?"

"Oh, a wonderfully gifted virtuoso. Simply remarkable."

"Is his violin called the Lamberti?"

"Ah . . . yes. Yes, it could well be. Makes sense."

"Where could I find Lamberti?"

A silence. "Playing in the great symphony in the sky, Mr. Fitzgerald."

"Dead?"

"Thirty or forty years ago."

It was a plot. Every time I traced the violin to somebody, the address was Queen of Heaven Cemetery.

15

I WALKED OUT of Van Leeb's, and for the first time I felt I was on the trail of that missing violin. Finally, I had a name: Gilberto Lamberti. All right, so he had been dead forty years; it was still better than nothing. Maybe.

And I had something else too. Hendrik Van Leeb, eminent luthier, had placed a Stradivarius in Erik Halvorsen's hands.

Retraction, my grumper!

I walked back up to Columbus Circle and kept going north to Lincoln Center. Through the little park across from O'Neal's Baloon, where a black statue of Dante stares down at you, through the courtyard with the fountain in the center in front of the Met, and along the right side to the library.

Inside, I was directed upstairs to the music library, and then came face-to-face with a young black woman who looked at me inquiringly.

"Uh ... I'm trying to find a violin ... a Stradivarius," I blurted out.

"You lost a Stradivarius?" She looked surprised.

"No, no. A book. Wait ... *The Iconography* ... *The Violin Iconography of Antonio Stradivari*." Finally.

In a few moments I was at a table, poring over a large gray-backed volume containing everything you ever wanted to know about Stradivari. There were photographs—front views, profiles, backs—in color, yet. And a listing of every known fiddle and every known owner.

I went down the list to the *L*'s, "Lamberti." There was a concise history of the instrument.

According to the *Iconography*, it was made by Stradivari in his workshop in Cremona, Italy, in 1722 when he was almost eighty years old. It was purchased by Count Brugen in Dresden and then by the Duke of Wexbourne, a relative of Queen Victoria, and given to the Earl of Andover. Then it passed to an American diplomat in Düsseldorf in 1860, was bought by a Chicago violin dealer in 1882, and sold to Angelo Lamberti that same year. Then it had passed to Gilberto Lamberti, the virtuoso. The current owner was listed as Jamison Lambert, New York City.

Back outside, I retraced my way past the Met and across the street into O'Neal's Baloon, wondering why the owners didn't know how to spell balloon.

I ordered a Schaefer and took it with me to the phone booth, where I got Jamison Lambert's number from information and dialed it.

"No, you haven't dialed the wrong number ... " a voice said.

"Hello ... ?"

" ... but there's no one here just now," it went on.

"What?" I said. Then I realized I was talking to one of those damned machines people hook up to their phones. I always want to talk back, but it's no use. I listened to the idiot voice drone on.

I was informed that if I wished to leave a message I could, after the beep, or if I wanted to reach Jason Lambert right away I could call another number.

Jason Lambert? I jotted the number down and dialed again.

"Hello ... Gondolier," somebody said.

It sounded like a live person, but I was still confused. "What?"

There was a little intake of breath. "Gondolier Limited. May I help you?"

"I'm trying to reach Jamison Lambert."

"Oh." There was a pause. "Well, I'm sorry, but Mr. Lambert has passed away."

I wasn't sure I had heard her correctly. "What?"

"Mr. Lambert is dead."

I stared at the phone and couldn't think of a thing to say. I mumbled, "Oh, sorry," and hung up.

It was a plot, all right! The Fates were playing cat and mouse with me. Here's Jamison. No, Jamison's gone. I walked back to the bar to sip the Schaefer.

"Why's balloon spelled wrong?" I asked the bartender for no particular reason.

"It isn't," he said. "They wanted to name it O'Neal's Saloon, but you can't name a saloon a saloon, so they made it baloon."

"Oh."

I wish I could say this helped anything at all.

I lighted a Tiparillo, sipped the beer, and let it all careen around inside my head. Gilberto Lamberti: R.I.P. Jamison Lambert: also R.I.P. Jason Lambert... I was lost in a goddam genealogical maze. Suddenly it came to me: Jason was the three-piece blond who had claimed the Lamberti at LaPorte's.

All I could think of was *"Avanti!"* Forward!

Back to the phone booth. I called the *Daily Press* library and got Margie.

"Hi, Margie, it's Fitz. Listen, have you got anything on a Jamison Lambert?"

"Let me check," she said.

In a minute she was back reading me a few clips. Jamison Lambert was the son of Gilberto Lamberti, a famous violinist, and a patron of the New York Philharmonic and the Metropolitan Youth Symphony Orchestra.

That rang a bell. What was it? Yes, the group Veronica Cerutti and Dennis Hanley played with.

"Anything else?"

"Well, he's dead. About two months ago."

"Yeah," I said. "Any heirs?"

"One nephew, named Jason."

"Any mention of a violin?"

"A violin?"

"A Stradivarius."

I heard papers rustling. "No . . . nothing like that."

Wonderful.

"I hate to ask you to check another one," I said, "but have you got an obit on a Gilberto Lamberti? Jamison's father?"

Margie obediently went back and dug out Gilberto's obituary for me. He had died in 1949.

"Any mention in the obit about a Stradivarius?"

Papers rustled. "No."

But I was on the scent now. I felt sure the Stradivarius Erik had shown us was the Lamberti. It had been at LaPorte's, and that's where Erik must have gotten it.

People sometimes wonder how a reporter chases a story. Well, that's how. You find something, and you keep following the string wherever it leads.

I drove downtown into SoHo, which is a cutesy name the shopowners have given to a neighborhood of lofts, boutiques, and art galleries south of Houston Street. Gondolier turned out to be a little import antique shop on Prince Street with a model of a Venetian Gondola in the window.

It was one of those places filled with Murano glass and statuary and leather goods and various bits of lace and other Italian and European items. The storefront shop appeared to have seen better days.

I went in and was greeted by a mousy-looking blonde in a red cardigan sweater with her glasses pushed up into her hair.

"I'm trying to find Jason Lambert."

The mousy blonde eagerly chirped, "Oh! Sure!" She

was polishing some kind of a brass lamp, but she put it down, went to the back, and stuck her head through a beaded curtain. I could hear low voices. Then Jason walked through the beads.

"Yes?" He gave me a shopkeeper's smile and walked toward me sunnily. It was the blond from LaPorte's. This time he was wearing a green jacket and had all the mannerisms of a clerk.

"Hi," I said. "Ed Fitzgerald, *Daily Press*. Remember me?"

Jason's alert eyes surveyed my face quickly, but nothing seemed to register.

I helped him. "I was at LaPorte's when you picked up your uncle's violin."

"Oh!" he examined me again. "Well...I'm afraid I didn't notice."

Wonderful to leave such an indelible impression.

"Your Uncle Jamison owned a Stradivari violin known as the Lamberti, right?"

Jason frowned at me. "That's correct."

"And now you have it?"

"That's right," he said stiffly. "It was left to me in his will. Why?"

I took out a Tiparillo and lighted it, studying the little Gondolier owner.

"There's something about that violin I don't understand," I told him.

"What's that?"

"Was your uncle trying to sell it?"

"Sell it?" Jason looked insulted.

"Had he commissioned LaPorte to find a buyer?"

Jason puffed up like a bullfrog. "Of course not. You don't sell something like that. It was left to him by his father, a very famous violinist."

"Do you know if the violin had been out of LaPorte's hands at all?" I tried again.

99

"Certainly not! My uncle put it in for servicing; you have to do that every so often. And it happened to still be there when he passed away."

That hit me. The Stradivarius was in LaPorte's hands when Jamison Lambert died.

"And then you claimed it when LaPorte... passed away," I finished idiotically.

"Yes. When I heard about Mr. LaPorte, I was frantic. But it was there."

"Mr. Lambert," I told him, "I think LaPorte was trying to sell that violin."

Jason glared at me. "That's quite impossible."

"You're quite sure your uncle didn't ask LaPorte to sell it? Did he need money, for instance?"

"I don't understand why you're asking these questions," he snipped, getting agitated. "This whole thing has been very upsetting."

I didn't blame him for being annoyed. I was annoyed too.

Jason must have been mulling it over, too. Because now he said, "Why do you think that?"

"Because somebody was trying to sell a Stradivari, and I think he got it from LaPorte, and I think it was the Lamberti."

Jason's face became pained at my first think and then derisive with the second one.

"You *think*?" he humphed. "Well, there's no way Mr. LaPorte could try to sell that violin, because he didn't own it. It doesn't make sense."

No, I agreed. It didn't make sense if LaPorte was operating on the level. But then somebody killed him. And that doesn't make sense, either.

"I've got another thought," I told Jason, and his face had that pained expression again.

"What?"

"See, LaPorte had your uncle's fiddle in his shop when the owner died. I think he decided that since your uncle wasn't coming back, he would sell it."

Jason gave me a sarcastic smile. "Mr. Fitzgerald, I have a thought, too," he said. "You're just looking for a story for that rag of yours."

He had me there.

"Well, I'm not interested in my uncle's name being dragged into this," he added. "Besides, he *didn't* sell it, did he? And the rightful owner has reclaimed it."

He had me again.

"The fact is that nothing has happened!" he concluded. "You're trying to make something out of nothing."

He had me once more.

No, nothing had happened. Only, two men had been killed for that nothing.

I left the little shop on Prince Street in SoHo and drove back uptown.

If you want to know how a reporter collapses on a story, that's how. You run out your string and you come to the end of it, and nothing's attached.

16

IT WAS LIKE that game you used to play in college, when somebody yells, "You can have all the beer you want!"

"Yay!"

"At ten bucks a glass."

"Boo!"

Except my game was all about the idiotic story I was chasing.

Van Leeb says Erik had a Stradivarius. "Yay!"

But it can't be found. "Boo!"

Erik had the Stradivarius when he was murdered. "Yay!"

But his violin wasn't even taken. "Boo!"

Erik got the Strad from LaPorte's. "Yay!"

But none were missing. "Boo!"

The game faded away as I drove and was replaced by a triangle floating in my mind, with Erik's face in the center. If I could connect up the three points around him and complete it, maybe I could figure it out. At one point, of course, was the damned pedigree violin.

Okay, Angle A: Erik had a Stradivarius. He showed it to all of us, to Cerutti, and finally to Van Leeb. Angle B: Erik didn't have a Stradivarius. Wilson said the one in Erik's apartment was just a regular fiddle. All right. Angle C: How the hell could I connect the angles when A and B were incongruent?

What it seemed to mean was that Erik had the Stradivarius before he was murdered, but afterward he only had his own fiddle.

And then the two geometric angles fitted, complementing each other. Of course! Wilson had said nothing was taken, and that's why there was no case. But something *was* taken—the Stradivarius. That's why Erik's own fiddle lay there in plain sight, undisturbed. Because the killer was looking for the Stradivarius, which Erik was carrying when he came in.

Suddenly, it all made sense. The fiddle case was open because the killer had looked at it and realized it wasn't what he wanted. The apartment was ransacked because the killer had been there searching for the Strad before Erik came home.

I felt elated as I drove into the NYP parking zone on East 40th Street. I had a feeling that uptown on East 82nd Street, Marcus Aurelius was smiling as he slept between the covers of *Meditations*. I had observed the movements of my own mind and had solved the triangle.

And then it occurred to me that I only had part of the triangle. I was satisfied in my own mind that Erik had had a Stradivarius and that somebody had killed him for it. But if it weren't the Lamberti, I still didn't know the name of the pompous violin or where it was or who had bloodied Erik's chest with six .25 caliber slugs.

Marcus's face floated before me again, and I saw that the smile was actually a smirk.

But at least I was able to write a story that a Queens businessman—Cerutti—had been shown a Stradivarius by Erik and that the luthier Van Leeb had authenticated it. I didn't use Cerutti's name, but I put in Van Leeb's. He hadn't told me anything in confidence.

I met Ariel after "Les Miserables" that night, and she was all agog to hear what had happened with Fred Cerutti. We sat at a table in Charlies and I told her about it.

"And Hendrik Van Leeb says it definitely was a Stradivarius?" she asked.

"Swears to it."

Ariel rolled her eyes. "Well, it must be so, then. He and Jacques Francais—and LaPorte, before he died—are just about the best-known experts in New York, and maybe in the world."

"So that means Hally really had one," I said. "Cerutti was buying it for his daughter, Veronica."

"Wait a minute," said Ariel. "Veronica Cerutti? She plays in the Metropolitan Youth Symphony Orchestra!"

"That's right," I said. "She knows your student, Dennis."

"Sure she would," said Ariel. "But if Hally was trying to sell a Stradivarius, which one was it?"

That was the jackpot question, all right.

"I'll tell you what I think. That it was one known as the Lamberti."

"The what?" Ariel perked up at that.

"The Lamberti. It was owned by a famous soloist, Gilberto Lamberti. Ever hear of him?"

"Of course."

"And the last owner was his son, Jamison Lambert."

Ariel put down her glass. "Wait a minute," she said. "Jamison Lambert? I know him."

"You do?"

"Yes! That is, I *knew* him. He was one of the main patrons of the youth orchestra. He gave Dennis a violin."

I lighted a Tiparillo. The threads were beginning to interweave, as they always do in a murder case. The trouble was finding them and then tracing them.

"When was this?"

"Before the last concert . . . in May. He always donated a fifteen-hundred-dollar scholarship to the orchestra in memory of his father, and there was an annual competition for it. In fact, it's called the Lamberti Competition."

"Go on."

This year, she said, Jamison had also given the orchestra a violin, which was to be played by the competition winner as long as he or she is in the orchestra.

"I know all about it, because Dennis won the competition," she said. "He was given a Scarampella. He's going to play it at the next concert in November."

A true friend of the youth orchestra was Jamison Lambert.

"What about Jason?" I asked.

"He's taken over for his uncle," she said. "He presented the Scarampella to Dennis, because Jamison died just before the concert."

"I see," I said, but of course I didn't.

I had dragged a Stradivari into the story, with the help of Cerutti and Van Leeb, and had been certain it was the Lamberti. Now, I didn't know.

And I certainly wasn't prepared for the reaction of Toupee Wilson. When I called him the next day from the office, he airily dismissed my scoop.

In the first place, he told me, he didn't give a Confederate damn about Van Leeb's opinion.

"The man looked at that violin for two seconds," he grumbled. "That's not scientific."

"Wilson, the man's an expert," I protested.

"Nobody's an expert in two seconds!"

And in the second place, he was more interested in the identity of the Queens businessman whose name I had left out.

"I got that name in confidence," I told him.

There was a pause. "I didn't think you took things in confidence," he sneered.

"Only when I have to," I said. "And I always regret it."

"I want that name," he raged.

For once, I was the one who didn't answer.

And in the third place, Wilson said, he didn't really care, because as far as he knew there was no Stradivarius in the case, and he was not in the business of speculation.

"Dammit, Wilson, the reason there was no Stradivarius

105

there is because it was stolen," I said. "Can't you see that?"

"That's your opinion."

"Marcus Aurelius says everything is opinion."

"Who?"

"Never mind. But I'm not printing a retraction."

Bang! *Errrrrrrrr* . . .

I didn't mind Wilson hanging up on me, though. I even understood. My story was forcing him to go back to work on Erik's murder instead of on others that might interest him more. I couldn't help it. It wasn't my fault that there are more than twelve hundred murders a year in New York and the cops can't handle the flow. If you want action on a case, you have to goose the cops. I was goosing.

I heard through the grapevine over the next few days that General Sherman, a.k.a. Toupee Wilson, was out there doggedly soldiering behind the lines again. Because Ariel called me all upset to tell me that she and everybody else were being questioned again.

"When is it going to stop?" she wailed.

I wanted to tell her it would stop when the killer was brought in, but I let it go.

I was out beating a few bushes myself. I hadn't put too much value in the Niagara twins' denunciation of Mitch Rogers as the probable killer, but I was interested in Mitch's slip in telling me about that fight.

I drove down into the Village again and stopped in at the White Horse Tavern, across from Erik's place. I sat at the bar, ordered a mug of stout, lighted a Tiparillo, and asked the bartender what he knew.

"Fitzgerald, *Daily Press*. Did you hear about that murder across the street on Eleventh?"

The bartender, a big blond guy wearing a bartender's apron, came over.

"Yeah! That violin player, Hally?"

"Did you know him?"

He nodded his big head slowly. "He used to come in sometimes. Pretty famous, huh?"

"Famous?"

"He was a soloist with the Philharmonic. Didn't you know that?"

"No. Who told you that?"

"He did. He didn't talk much about it, though, you know? You know how these famous guys are. They don't have to."

"Yeah. Did you hear anything about a fight over there that night?"

The bartender leaned against the bar. "You know, I think the night bartender saw it. And some of the customers."

"Really?"

"Yeah, the cops were around asking questions."

"Do you know what he told them?"

"Jeez, I only heard it secondhand. But it was about the girl they were fighting over, I understand."

"Girl? There was a girl there?"

"Sure. I think so. Nick noticed the car too. A big Mercedes."

I sipped my stout and took a puff on the Tiparillo. A girl? Ingrid? But Mitch said he had dropped her off first.

"Do you have any idea what she looked like?"

He shook his head. "Now you've got me there, reporter. Why don't you come around later and talk to Nick?"

I told him I would, but as it turned out I never got the chance.

I kept calling Detective Wilson to find out if he was making any progress, but he never returned my calls. I should have been suspicious, I guess, but what could I have done anyway?

Well, as I found out later, Wilson and Nickerson talked to Hendrik Van Leeb, and questioned everybody again, and talked to the people around the White Horse too.

Because the next thing I heard, Wilson had made an arrest and cleaned up the whole case. He arrested Mitch Rogers for killing Erik.

I found out when I read my damned story in the *New York Post* and in the *Times*.

17

IT'S BAD ENOUGH to read your story in the opposition, but that's never the end of it. You still have to write a follow, a day late, and try to make it look fresh. And you have to listen to the ravings of your city editor.

"Fitz," Ironhead said, as though to a fourth-grader, "you have to learn to cultivate contacts in this business."

"Yes, sir."

"You can't go around antagonizing detectives who are the source of good stories."

Then I had to crawl back to Detective Wilson at the West 10th Street station and get the facts.

Oddly enough, Toupee Wilson was effusive and ready to talk. I guess he was just tickled pink to make me look like a first-class jerk, and he obviously relished the fact that I had to write the story as he gave it to me.

He even had the nerve to tell me that the *Post* just happened to call him for a fill-in just when he was bringing in a rather bewildered Mitch Rogers. He didn't know how the *Times* found out.

"You know Milt Nathanson, don't you?"

I had to say I did.

"He called and hopped right over here. Listen, I didn't have time to give the story out. You should have been here."

"Yeah," I said.

That's the way it is with detectives and reporters. You know you have to meet again on another story one of these days, and you have to keep the lines of communication open. If he crowed about savaging me and the *Daily Press*, he knew we might get even one day.

Anyway, he had arrested Mitch Rogers "as the result of police investigation," and the crime had nothing to do with a Stradivarius, stolen or otherwise, as he had tried to tell me a million times before.

"Okay. So what's it all about?"

"First," he said, making a little circle on his yellow pad, "he had the opportunity. He was the last person with him."

He made another circle around the first one. "Second, he had a motive, the oldest motive in the world. Jealousy."

"What?" I asked.

"He and the victim both wanted the same woman."

"You mean Ingrid Sohn?"

He darted a look at me. "I'm afraid I can't go into that."

Another circle was forming around the first two on the yellow pad. "I also know that Mitch Rogers was universally hated by all musicians."

"That's just because he's a contractor," I told him. "All fiddlers hate all contractors. Something like the way cops feel about reporters."

Wilson laughed, showing a little strain.

"Anything more?" I pressed him.

He nodded. "Yes. Discrepancies in Rogers's statements."

"Such as what?"

I would get no details about that, he told me. Only that Rogers had given "inconsistent" accounts of himself. The facts would come out in court.

"I don't intend to try this case in the press," he concluded unctuously.

"Did you recover the gun?" I asked, and Wilson reacted with annoyance. "Not yet."

"And of course you're not looking for the violin."

"What violin?"

"The Stradivarius that's missing."

"There is no missing violin except in your imagination."

Wilson crumpled up the yellow pad with the target on it and dumped it into a tin waste can beside his desk. That, he suggested, was all he needed for the moment.

"This case is disposed of, as far as the department is concerned," he pronounced.

Wonderful.

The story I wrote wasn't much, I'm afraid. Second-day catch-up stories seldom are. The only good thing about it was that it was over, and Ariel Ryan could relax and forget about it. After I finished work, I met her for coffee at the Indian place near the Winter Garden. That's all you find in Manhattan these days, it seems: Indians. From India, that is, not from Arizona. The guy who runs the newsstand in the subway is a Hindu from Bombay, and the guy who serves you coffee near the Winter Garden is a Sikh from Punjab.

I wanted to talk to her before she went in to play "Les Miserables" so I could bring her up to date. She was relieved, all right.

"I wouldn't have thought it of Mitch"—she sighed—"but then, who would you think it of?"

"Yeah," I agreed.

"What happened, do you know?"

"Apparently, they tripped Mitch up on his story," I told her. "I'm not surprised. He was a little shaky when he talked to me."

"Tripped him up about what?"

"Ingrid, I think. I thought Hally was going with Ingrid."

Ariel blushed a little. We hadn't ever really talked about her and Hally.

It was complicated, she said, as romance often is. Mitch and Ingrid had started seeing each other even when Mitch was still married.

"His marriage was a shambles already," said Ariel. "Ingrid didn't cause it."

Then Mitch had gone back to his wife, trying to work it out. And, as sometimes happens, that had led to a real split. Mitch had moved out for good, but by then Ingrid was seeing Hally.

"When Mitch came back, he and Ingrid took up again, that's all," said Ariel. "But Hally was pretty burned up. Hally was usually the one who walked out, you see."

I looked into my coffee.

"Is that what happened with the two of you?" I said, not wanting to ask but unable to stop myself.

She nodded. "More or less. He had big ideas. I wanted to quit the rat race. He wanted to be the chief rat."

I let it drop.

"But anyway"—she brightened—"we can put it behind us now."

"I guess so."

"I talked to those people in Vermont," she went on. "They want me to come up for an interview."

"That's great!"

Ariel smiled. "Isn't it? I've been thinking about it all day. Imagine... away from all this insanity. Where'd you say you're from, St. Louis?"

"Yes."

She smiled. "That's why you're too basic for New York."

I didn't quite get that. But I understood what she meant about New York being insane. It's a constant battle. No matter what you want to do, somebody wants to do the opposite. No matter which way you're going, somebody's going the other way. And no matter where you want to go, you can't get there on time.

"Is that what you really want?" I asked her.

She smiled. "Oh, yes. It's what I've always wanted."

"So why are you here?"

Ariel looked out onto Broadway wistfully. "I don't know, Fitz. I guess I got caught up in it. When I finished at Juilliard, I decided to stay on for a while. And a while keeps dragging on, and I'm still here."

"Yeah." Her explanation was why most of the people in New York live their whole lives here.

But now she was ready to get out. Something had happened to the dream, whatever it was. She was not going to be a soloist at Avery Fisher Hall. She was good, very good. She might even eventually get a chair in the violin section of the New York Philharmonic or the Met, although those chances became slimmer with each passing year. But even if that happened, there would still be the great snake pit of New York City to wade through daily.

Erik's murder had been the last straw, she told me. The horrible reality that everyone fears. And then, too, her apartment building was going co-op.

"Fitz, I can't afford to live here anymore," she said. "Not in Manhattan. I don't know, it's all just too much."

So, there it was, Ariel Ryan's valedictory.

I couldn't blame her.

She was smiling enticingly. "You want to drive up to Vermont with me?"

"Sure," I said.

So that's how it came about that I went to Vermont. I took two days off, and we drove north on the New York Thruway, up through the rolling wooded hills of the Catskills to Lake George. We spent the night at Lake George, in a place called the Wagon Wheel Motel, set in fir trees on the lower tip of the lake.

Sitting outside on the porch with a Schaefer and a white wine, we gazed up at the wheeling constellations in the sky, a magnificent sight commonplace to those who live in the Adirondacks, but invisible from Manhattan or the Bronx.

"Isn't it wonderful up here?" she whispered.

Well, of course it was. With Ariel in my arms that night and the smell of the pine trees coming in the windows, New York and its headaches were nonexistent.

The next day we were up early to head north again, up through Ticonderoga, to Lake Champlain, and finally to Burlington. Then we headed deeper into Vermont, past Winooski and Mount Mansfield, going by great icebergs of granite outcroppings, which is why Vermont is called the Granite State. And then there was Allen, Vermont, and Allen State College, snuggled in a green campus.

I looked around at a foreign country. Was it Ireland? Was it Norway? It sure as hell wasn't the Big Apple.

We strolled around the campus hand in hand, looking at the buildings and going through the auditorium where Ariel would lead the string department if she took the job.

Ariel had her interview Monday morning while I drove into the town of Allen, which didn't amount to even Glendale in Queens. And like a busman on holiday, what did I do but walk into the *Allen World*, the local newspaper on Johnson Street in the center of town.

"Yes, sir!" A man looked up from a desk and then walked over to the counter.

"Oh, uh. Hello." That from me in an outburst of explanation.

"What can I do for you?" the *Allen World* man asked.

I realized there was nothing he could do for me.

"Well"—I blushed—"I just happened to be passing through. I'm a reporter from New York."

"Oh!" he said. "Oakley . . . Terry Oakley."

I shook hands. "Ed Fitzgerald. *New York Daily Press*."

He nodded his head. "Big paper. So. Just passing through, huh?"

"Yeah. A friend of mine might be moving up here."

"That so?"

"She might be the new head of the string department at the college."

Terry Oakley looked out the window toward the college, then back at me. He was a tall slim guy with horn-rimmed glasses, wearing a corduroy jacket.

"What's her name?" he asked.

"Ariel Ryan. She's from New York too."

"I heard they were looking for somebody," said Oakley. He was jotting down notes.

"What are you doing?" I asked, surprised.

"Well, now, Fitzgerald, that's a pretty good story up here, you know. New string department head at the college."

I'm afraid I chuckled a little. Oakley shot a glance at me.

"I'm sorry," I told him. "I see what you mean. It's just that in New York it isn't usually a story unless there's a dead body or two."

Oakley smiled. "Yeah. I worked in Boston. I know."

"Boston? The *Globe*?"

"Yep. Came up here ten years ago. Love it." He waved me toward the end of the counter. "Come on in ... have a look."

He walked back into the printshop, a nice, compact little operation. I picked up a copy of the *World*, which is a small circulation daily.

"Yep," said Oakley, "we're pretty basic in our news up here. Hatch, match, and dispatch."

I looked at him. "What's that?"

Oakley chuckled. "You big shots never heard that? Why, that's births, marriages, and deaths."

I looked out toward the street. "Nice little town," I said.

"Oh, yes." He smiled. "Henny and I love it. She's kind of left the operation to me now, since the twins came along."

Well, Terry Oakley insisted on walking me across the street and down to the Northway Restaurant, where the Rotary Club met for lunch.

"We got an Elks Club, too," he told me pointedly.

Well.

He also told me that his wife, Henrietta, had her hands full with three young children at home, and that he was running the *Allen World* alone. There was Anna, who did

115

the classifieds, and Homer, the printer, and some college kids to help out. But what he really needed was another good newspaperman to be managing editor.

I looked at him and lighted a Tiparillo.

"That is, if you and your friend were thinking of moving up here."

Is that what I was thinking of? Because Terry Oakley's words brought it out onto the table. Is that what was happening? I thought of Ariel, her delicate perfection, her need to make a home somewhere away from the madness of New York.

I guess that's how decisions are made and how you change your life. I stared out the window of the Northway at the green hills of Allen, Vermont. No dirty subways, no berserk, shoving crowds of people, no clogged Seventh Avenue full of honking yellow taxis. No, outside was an orderly world, with Hathaway's Antique Shoppe, the Granite Book Nook, and a white-painted little grocery store: a tidy street with New England signs swinging above the stores, black printing on white. I was in Thoreau country, and it was wonderful.

Ariel and I, settled down in Vermont? With Ariel on the faculty at Allen College, we would have entrée to some interesting people. I could finally write that novel I was always threatening to start. And a job as managing editor on the *Allen World*, without dead bodies around every corner, with no beslavering Ironhead Matthews, without the endless grinding, energy-consuming hassle of daily life in the Big Apple.

Marcus Aurelius might have said we had reached the Happy Isles.

I told Terry Oakley I'd think about it and then went to pick up Ariel.

She walked out of the administration building demurely, smiling just so, like a Junior League debutante in *Town and Country*, and it wasn't until I'd driven through town on

Johnson Street that she let out a victorious whoop.

"They want me!"

I pulled over and she hurtled into my arms again, hugging me and laughing. "Fitz, they want me!"

"Of course they do," I said. "Who wouldn't?"

All the way back down through Winooski and Burlington and south again toward New York, Ariel bubbled along about what life would mean in Vermont. It would be all apple cider and Mozart in Robert Frost country. Being head of the string department there would mean something, she pointed out.

"Not like New York, where there are violinists climbing in through every window, each one better than the last. You can never relax in New York. It's always a struggle."

"You're not the only one with news," I finally told her.

"What? What do you mean?"

"I got a job offer at the *Allen World*."

Ariel looked at me, her eyes wide. "Really?"

I nodded.

"Fitz!" I had to pull over into a rest stop so she could throw herself into my arms. "But, that means ... Fitz, I can't tell you how happy I am!" And she gave me a Wagnerian kiss.

We drove south through the day, and the closer we got to New York, the more Vermont seemed like the Emerald City. The marvelous wooded hills of upstate gradually disappeared as we reached the suburbs in Rockland County, and the spell twinkled out as we rolled with a grind across the metal grid of the George Washington Bridge back into the real world. From the bridge, you can see all the way down the Hudson River to the World Trade Center towers. There it was again, the city of bridges.

18

I WOKE UP the next morning and realized I was not a prisoner anymore. I had a woman to love and a job offer in Vermont. I had fantasized many times about how I would quit the idiotic life of the *Daily Press*, a dream usually connected with winning the New York Lottery for five million dollars. Or as the result of a best-seller I had knocked off between murders and obits.

In my fantasy, I would walk to the city desk, climb up on top of it over Ironhead's wondering gaze, and with great deliberation pee in all directions.

Imagine, a quiet life in Vermont, with time enough to read and write and actually listen to music and conversation. And, who knows, with Oakley and the *Allen World*, I might even eventually be able to buy into it.

It was a dream shared by endless ink-stained wretches in New York, who become reporters looking for adventure and glamour and find what Fred Allen once called a treadmill to oblivion. Reporters aiming at becoming the next Theodore H. White wind up covering politics in Brooklyn. Crusaders looking to topple City Hall find themselves covering fires and purse-snatchings.

Some get out, of course, to become flacks for the Water Commissioner or some other politician. Others drift from beat to beat, trapped in the inertia of the job. But they can't quit the newspaper business, just as the guy following an elephant with a shovel and a wheelbarrow can't imagine giving up the wonderful world of the circus.

Well, not me. I wasn't going to wind up hump-backed

and gray-headed on the copy desk. I was going someplace where being a newspaperman meant something, where good work was rewarded. Allen, Vermont.

I lay in bed for a while, smoking a Tiparillo and luxuriating in my newfound freedom and independence. Oh, wouldn't Ironhead squeal when his best street reporter walked out!

I had cleaned up the Halvorsen murder story, and there was nothing to hold me now.

I flipped on the radio and made some coffee, still sailing in my wondrous, liberated mood. There: it was WQXR and Schubert's *Unfinished Symphony*. I could listen to that all the time in Vermont, away from the clatter and squealing taxis outside my window. I could drive along without being honked at by maniacs and park the damned car like a human being.

Schubert's symphony played on, as though just for me. I would learn more about classical music, being with Ariel.

And why hadn't Schubert finished that piece? I wondered. Something else unfinished was trying to ease its way into my mind. I remembered a story about a woman found dead in her bed in Co-Op City with a bullet in her. The cops concluded somebody had fired a shot at random from the roof of another building and killed the poor woman.

So what did that have to do with me? Just that it was unfinished, too. They knew the end of it, the poor dead woman, but not the beginning: who had fired the shot. I had the end of the Halvorsen murder, the arrest of Mitch Rogers, but not the beginning. Drinking coffee and thinking of Vermont, I kept woolgathering about that damned missing violin that wasn't missing. That's what happens to reporters when they wrap up a story but can't stop worrying it.

What the hell. It was disposed of.

When I got to the office that day, I checked with the

Manhattan District Attorney's office about Mitch Rogers. There would be a bail hearing later in the day in Criminal Court, an A.D.A. told me.

Well, maybe the loose ends would be tied up then. Because at a bail hearing some of the case against a defendant has to be put on the record, so the judge can decide how much bail to set, or whether to refuse bail altogether.

I told Ironhead I'd drop down to Criminal Court for the bail hearing, which would probably be my last story on the case. After that, it would drift into the province of the court reporters.

I called Ariel, and her voice came over the phone like a symphony of her own.

"How's the Granite State princess?" I asked.

"The *what?*" She laughed. "Fitz, I hope you aren't going sappy on me." But then she admitted the idea of escape was filling her world too.

"There's only one last story for me to do," I told her. "After that—"

Then it popped out.

"Say, I've been wondering. Where do you think Hally could have gotten his hands on that Stradivarius if it didn't come from LaPorte's?"

Ariel reacted in a funny way. She said, "What?" but it was really silence.

"See, it's a loose end—"

"What are you talking about, Fitz? I thought it was all over."

"Well, yes, except that no violin has turned up."

"But his violin was *there*."

I tried to explain that Erik had definitely had a Stradivari at one point.

Real silence this time.

"Well, maybe I'll find out at the bail hearing," I said.

"I don't want to hear anymore about it," she said levelly. "They've got Mitch, and that's it."

I told her I'd call later and hung up. I understood, all right. People can't stand loose ends, especially threatening ones. Ariel needed a solution just as much as Toupee Wilson.

I drove my coughing Monte Carlo down the FDR Drive to Foley Square for the bail hearing.

I was just in time for lunch at Giambone's, the Italian restaurant behind the Criminal Court Building on Mulberry Street where I'd spent many an instructive afternoon at the elbow of judges, lawyers, and Harry Reeves, the *Post* reporter who covered Manhattan Supreme Court.

"Well, if it isn't Fitzboggen," yelped Reeves when I walked in. He called me that, he said, because "all you Irishers are out of the peat bogs."

"Hey, you old fart," I greeted him.

Of course I had to have a couple of Schaefers while Reeves devoured some bombs—martinis.

"So what brings you down here, hotshot?" he wanted to know.

I told him.

"Wait a minute," said Reeves gravely, lifting his florid face to study some far-off recollection. "Is this the story that the *Post* stole from under your bungling nose?"

Terrific.

"Yes," he went on, letting his table companions in on it—two lawyers and a judge—"here we have Fitzboggen, the dreadnought of the *Daily Press*, who can find a story inside his own pants every time, as long as it bites him on the grumper."

"Thanks," I said.

Reeves's high, needling cackle filled Giambone's. So the damned case was also spreading my fame around town as a hopeless nincompoop.

I walked across the Chinatown playground to the back door of the Criminal Court Building, flanked by the somber Tombs prison, and inside into the bedlam. I walked through to the lobby and banged on the door of the pressroom. You can't just walk into pressrooms anymore, because reporters have to lock them against the myriad schools of crazies overflowing the lobby.

Mickey Pearl of the *Post* opened the door a crack and let me in. "Hey, Fitz." He beamed. "Nice story you gave us the other day."

"You're welcome."

Mickey and the *Daily Press* reporter, Jimmy Swanson, checked the calendars for me to see where the bail hearing would be.

"You covering that?" Swanson asked, willing to get out of it.

"Yeah," I said.

Mickey and I strolled down the scarred corridor to A.P. One to the bail hearing, and who did I see about to go into the courtroom but Ingrid Sohn, the squinty violist.

"Ingrid."

She halted as though frozen, apparently bewildered at hearing her name in this strange, gloomy place.

"You're the reporter?" she asked uncertainly, drawing back from the door.

"Yeah. Come here a minute." I walked her over into a corner, hoping to pump her for some information. She was the one person who had been at the Algonquin bar whom I had not talked to.

Ingrid was already lighting up a cigarette with shaky hands, squinting at me nervously. What was she doing here? seemed to be her message. Mine too.

"This is so awful," she gasped. "How can they do this to Mitch? Somebody has to help him." Her look into my eyes left no doubt who she thought that person should be.

"You don't think he did it?"

"I know he didn't," she said earnestly. "I was with him the whole time!"

I looked at her. "The cops say he changed his story."

Ingrid leaned against the wall. She was crying. "Of course he changed it, the poor, silly fool. He lied the first time... to protect me."

"Why protect you?"

Ingrid talked like a wooden mannequin, the story pouring out of her nonstop. She and Mitch had taken Hally home that night and told him they were going back together.

"He was furious... crazy drunk. He could hardly walk. He was yelling, trying to hit Mitch. Mitch had to help him inside. I stayed in the car."

But, she went on, when they heard about the murder, Mitch Rogers tried to keep her out of things by telling the police he was alone. He still had an alibi, because he went directly to Ingrid's.

"I told the cops what he wanted me to," she said.

But it didn't stop. When my stories kept appearing, the police came back. They questioned her and Mitch again, and this time Mitch got confused.

"When he told them the truth, they didn't believe him," she said. "Now they say he did it, and I'm covering up for him. They say if I don't testify against him, they'll charge me too." She dragged on her cigarette. "They don't believe either of us now."

I studied her. I was having the same problem. Had they both lied the first time, or were they lying now?

We walked into A.P. One, which was about half filled with the struggle of street people and bewildered defendants you find down there. Court officers and A.D.A.s and Legal Aid Society lawyers milled around, going over calendars and checking papers. It's very difficult for the casual observer to make much sense of things.

I went up past the railing into the well of the court and checked with the harried court clerk. He went over the calendar and found *People v. Rogers*. It would be coming up pretty soon, he said.

After a while, the door to the holding pens opened and the defendants drifted in to sit on a long bench against the far wall. As their names were called by the clerk, they got up and walked over to stand before the judge.

Finally, I saw Mitch. He looked like something out of a concentration camp. Absolutely pole-axed. A man went over to chat, squatting down before him as Mitch sat on the long bench. It had to be the Legal Aid Society lawyer assigned to him, and those few minutes were all the consultation Mitch would get.

Then Mitch was brought before the judge.

"*People versus Rogers*," said the judge, shuffling papers. "Is there an application?"

Up stepped the Legal Aid lawyer and asked for Mitch's release on personal recognizance, which meant without bail.

Then the A.D.A. "Your honor, the defendant is charged with second-degree murder. The people recommend he not be admitted to bail."

That finally caught the attention of the judge, who had been wading through papers on the bench. He looked down at the A.D.A.

"Please, Mr. Davies," he said in exasperation. "May we for once dispense with the impossible?"

"Five hundred thousand dollars," said the A.D.A.

The judge sighed, took off his glasses, and studied the forlorn face of one Mitchell Rogers, contractor and suspect, sometimes known as the most dishonest person in the history of Local 802.

"Let's hear it," the judge said.

The A.D.A. launched into his argument as to why Mitch should be held under lock and key until the trial. "The defendant's residence is in New Jersey," he explained, which meant he might not return to the jurisdiction of New York County. The defendant had no means of his own to post bond, because the Mercedes he drove was owned by his mother.

I glanced at Ingrid in the spectators' seats. She was shaking her head at this public embarrassment.

Then the Legal Aid lawyer, who looked to be about twenty-four, argued that his client denied the charge and that the case against him was circumstantial.

"Bail is set at twenty thousand," the judge said tiredly. "Next matter, please."

Afterward, Ingrid and Mitch talked in low whispers at the courtroom rail for a few minutes, and then they took him away, back out into the bullpen, where he would catch the Department of Correction van back to Rikers Island.

When Ingrid walked out of court, I caught up with her.

"I've got to get him out," she muttered. "His mother didn't even show up. All she has is her house, and she said she won't put that up."

As soon as we were out in the corridor, she lighted a cigarette and leaned against the wall as though exhausted.

"Fitzgerald," she said, "you've got to tell those cops Mitch didn't do it. You know them."

I sighed. Did I know Detective Wilson?

"They won't listen to me," I told her. "They needed somebody to arrest."

"But it's crazy," she said urgently. "Mitch had no reason. There was nothing for him to be jealous about. We were back together. Somebody else killed Hally, Fitz. It's got to be about that damned Stradivarius."

My ears perked up. "Why do you say that?"

"I was going with Hally for a while. There's something funny about that violin. That's why LaPorte was killed."

"The cops say there's no connection."

Ingrid let out smoke disdainfully. "Jesus." She looked at me with a sneer. "Hally got a Stradivarius from LaPorte. He told me so."

"What?"

"Yes. And it's a phony or something. LaPorte was a crook. Anybody will tell you that. He'd swear anything was a Stradivarius if he could get away with it. Hally was trying to sell it for LaPorte. I tried to warn him. Now I realize why he wouldn't listen."

"Why?"

"He was in on it! He and LaPorte! They were going to clean up."

"Do you know who he was trying to sell it to?" I asked.

Her head wagged. "He wouldn't tell me. By that time, we were hardly speaking. I was afraid something would happen, but . . . not Mitch."

Suddenly, she hurried away down the corridor. I had the sensation that somebody was watching me, and when I glanced up I saw I was right: Toupee Wilson and Nickerson.

They walked over. "What'd she say?" Wilson wanted to know.

I shook my head. I wasn't going to get into the middle again.

"Satisfied?" he said then. "The guy's lying through his teeth. He went in with Halvorsen and shot him."

I didn't know what to say. I had to admit they had a case, and maybe, like Ariel, I wanted a solution too. I was sick and tired of the whole thing, and besides, there was another life waiting for me now.

Back down the corridor to the pressroom. I called in the bail hearing story, but Glenn the switchboard guy intercepted me.

"Fitz? Hey, listen, that broad called again."

"What broad?"

"Ariel Ryan?"

"About what?"

"She was pretty wired, Fitz. Said she's been robbed or something."

"Robbed?"

"That's what she said. Somebody broke into her apartment."

19

I'M CONSIDERABLY FUZZY about the next half hour. I know that I called Ariel and she told me over the phone in terrified little half breaths that somebody had broken in and that the cops were with her. I know I ran to my Monte Carlo and drove down around the Battery and up the West Side to her place on Riverside Drive.

Up in the slow elevator and into her apartment. I noticed the door was splintered.

Inside there were two uniformed cops talking to her as she sat huddled on the sofa, a bag of groceries still in her arms. She dropped them and ran to me.

"Fitz!"

"What happened?"

Ariel didn't know, she said. Only that she had been out shopping and had come home to find the door splintered and standing ajar. She had fled and called the police and only entered when they did.

The apartment was in a shambles, papers strewn all over, blown out of her desk as though a cyclone had passed.

The two cops seemed relived to see me. They wanted to get out of there, it was clear.

"We'll make a report," the older, gray-headed one said gently.

"Anything missing?" I asked.

He shook his head. "The lady says she doesn't know."

The two cops left, and Ariel stood there pressed against me holding my hands with talons and wouldn't let go. And a professional violinist has powerful hands.

I finally unclasped her fingers and sat her down at a table in the small kitchen off the living room, away from the devastation.

She looked at me wide-eyed, bewildered. I found myself pacing in the tiny kitchen, back and forth, a Tiparillo in my teeth. I halted at the small gas range and put on the tea kettle. When it whistled, I made tea, put a cup in front of her, and sat at the table with her.

"Now, listen," I told her. "It could be a burglar."

"I know."

"But it could be about . . . "

"It has to be, Fitz." She was calmer now, even stoical. I saw control move into her face. Discipline was something she understood.

"What would anybody want with me?" she said, and she was thinking hard.

We exchanged glances, and we both knew what it was about.

"It's got to be about Hally," she finally said. "Fitz, the killer must have been here."

I got up and walked into the living room, surveying the music sheets and stationery on the floor around her desk. She followed, holding her tea.

"What was he looking for?" I asked.

It occurred to me that I had seen the same scene at Erik's when he was found dead, and at LaPorte's as well.

"Somebody has been looking for something at all three places," I said, and Ariel shuddered. I hadn't meant to equate this burglary with the two murders, but there it was.

She began picking up the papers, first the music sheets, which she carefully arranged, then the other papers. Deftly, she thumbed through them, shaking her head.

"I don't know," she murmured miserably. "I just don't know. If anything's missing, I don't know what it is."

She sat on the sofa and drew her legs up under her. I kept pacing.

Thoughts and ideas swirled around in my head. If it were about Erik's murder, and *if* the cops were right, then it had to be about Mitch Rogers. Except that Mitch was on Rikers Island.

But if it were about Erik, and it had to be, and it wasn't about Mitch, and it couldn't be, it was back to square one.

That damned Stradivarius.

"Is there anything about Hally you haven't told me?"

She thought it over. "No . . . nothing. We went together. He had big ideas and wouldn't hear of leaving New York."

I let that go through me.

"He wanted to be a contractor, and he said he had that violin to sell, and . . . I just don't know."

"Have you ever had anything to do with a Stradivarius yourself?"

"No," said Ariel. She had looked at them, but had never so much as touched one. She had seen the one Erik was carrying around, and she had seen the one Jamison Lambert sometimes brought to rehearsals of the Metropolitan Youth Symphony Orchestra, she said.

"The Lamberti," I said.

"Yes."

I had traced Erik's violin as far as Hendrik Van Leeb, and after that it had vanished.

I had traced the second one as far as Jason Lambert, and he had it.

I could think of no other directions to pursue. And yet there was still somebody out there on a pursuit of his own, somebody who killed Erik and LaPorte and fired three shots at me.

You know what frustration is? It's when you have to do something but don't know how to do it. You know what frustration leads to? Anxiety.

It all went weaving through my head, like the interweav-

129

ing strains of a symphony. Which was the theme? Since I was not a reincarnation of Richard Wagner, or even a pimple on his bassoon, I had to plod along one note at a time.

It was Schubert's *Unfinished Symphony* again, sailing mockingly through my untutored mind. What was it? Something about these interlocking threads led to the Gordian knot I had to cut.

I asked Ariel if she would be all right there alone, and she looked at me as though I had invited her to sit on top of the Chernobyl reactor.

"Are you crazy? I'm not staying here alone!"

So she packed a bag, and we drove across town through the 86th Street Central Park transverse to my place. Sorry as I was about her scare, there were worse things than having Ariel Ryan move in with you.

"Fitz," she said, "let's get out now."

"What?"

"Let's go to Vermont. The hell with all this."

"Ariel, there's nothing I'd rather do."

She fixed those steady eyes upon me and waited for the unspoken "but" at the end of my sentence.

"But I have to clear this up first," I told her.

She just kept looking.

"We can't go with this hanging over us..."

Her look was long and steady, and there were unspoken words in it, too.

20

I DON'T WANT you to think I'm comparing ink-stained wretches to Ludwig van Beethoven, but it occurs to me that reporters go about their trade much as did Ludwig. They tell the story of the ambitious student who came to Beethoven for help in becoming a composer. When the great man suggested the fledgling begin with an étude, the *jungen* declared, "I want to start with a symphony, like you."

Yes, replied Ludwig, he had started with a major work, "But I didn't ask anyone how to do it."

That's the way it is with reporters. Ludwig couldn't wait until he knew how to write a symphony to begin. He plunged in. A reporter can't wait either. I had to plunge ahead.

I became a Johnny One Note, my eye fixed upon a single target: the Lamberti Stradivarius. It had to be the answer. Soon the *Unfinished Symphony* segued into something else: the Lamberti Sonata. I can't give you the melody, but it's probably something that would have caused old Ludwig to be happy that he was as deaf as a post.

Anyway, I went after the Lamberti, which meant pursuing Gilberto, his son, Jamison Lambert, and Jason. Gilberto had left it to Jamison, and Jamison had taken it to LaPorte. Jason had picked it up later. Somehow, during the time LaPorte had it, the violin had gotten into Erik's hands. But LaPorte had it again when he was killed. I wonder if it's that difficult to write a lousy symphony?

Actually, my target was the one who had the Lamberti now. Jason. And the only connection I could find between him and Ariel was the Metropolitan Youth Symphony.

I found the youth orchestra office in Carnegie Hall in a broom closet halfway up a staircase. Carnegie Hall has a regular rabbit warren of rooms and studios for musicians that most people don't even know about.

The office wasn't much: a desk, some filing cabinets, and posters on the wall. What the organization does is stage four concerts in Carnegie Hall each year in which the best metropolitan-area high school musicians perform, so it doesn't really need a lot of office space or a big staff. The staff is the parents of the musicians, I discovered.

Anyway, the person who held it all together was Rudolph Oppitz, the orchestra manager, who looked up when I found his broom-closet office and walked in.

"Fitzgerald, *Daily Press*," I told him.

Oppitz stood up behind his desk and shoved out his hand.

"Rudolph Oppitz!" he said with a smile. "I was hoping you could make it."

"Pardon me?"

"Karen said she'd called the *Daily Press*. How can I help you?"

I sighed and sat down. So did Oppitz. The rule about the press was in operation, as usual. If the guy you're talking to is an orchestra manager, he thinks you must be an arts and entertainment writer come to do a piece about his orchestra.

I wish I could tell you I disabused him of that notion right away. But I sort of let it slide for the moment, because he seemed eager to talk. And I wanted some answers.

"I'm curious about Jamison Lambert," I offered.

"Mr. Lambert?" He seemed surprised. "Well! He was a wonderful man, a great friend of the orchestra. You want to do a story about him?"

"I don't know," I stalled. "I understand he supported your organization."

Oppitz leaned back in his creaky swivel chair and put his fingertips together. He nodded slowly, sadly. "Yes ... yes ... for many years." He frowned.

"What can you tell me about him?"

Rudolph Oppitz, a pudgy man with a bald dome, sat forward and gathered his wits. Jamison Lambert had been a pillar of the orchestra, he said. A member of the board, a tireless helper, a contributor.

"You know, his father, Gilberto Lamberti, was one of the great violinists," he said.

"So I've heard. Did Jamison play too?"

Oppitz raised his right hand and waggled it, suggesting uncertain success. "*Mezzo, mezzo,*" he said. "Not like his father."

"But Jamison was a violinist?"

Oppitz's waggling hand paused and then made a forced descent to his desk. He let out a long breath.

"Well, no. Not professionally. He enjoyed sitting in with the orchestra at rehearsals sometimes."

"Oh."

"He would sit in the violin section, at the end of a row, and play along," said Oppitz.

"What else can you tell me?"

Well, Oppitz could tell me plenty. "Are you interested in the Lamberti Competition? Is that it? We tried to get the press to write about it, but all they want to do are stories about Juilliard," he complained.

"So, tell me about it."

Well, he launched in, every year the Youth Orchestra held a competition for the violin sections, in which the prize was a $1,500 scholarship from Jamison Lambert in memory of his father.

"It was his most important contribution, you know, other than the support he gave by his name and his devotion."

Well, this year, Jamison had gone even further.

"I guess he knew he was failing, you know," said Oppitz. "We lost him a couple of months back."

"Yes, I know."

He brightened again. "This year, Mr. Lambert contributed a violin to the orchestra for the winner to play."

I sat forward. "Was that the Scarampella given to Dennis Hanley?"

"Yes. Would you like to talk to Dennis? I could easily arrange it."

"Well," I hedged. "I don't know."

Oppitz watched me. "Is there something in particular . . . ?"

"I'll tell you, Mr. Oppitz. What I'm wondering about is Mr. Lambert's own violin. A Stradivarius known as the Lamberti."

Oppitz frowned and his face flushed. A shadow slid over his features. "What about it?" he asked defensively.

"Do you know anything about it?"

Oppitz looked down at his desk, then back at me. "I don't know how you found out about this, but I'm afraid I can't actually confirm anything," he said somberly.

"Well, that's all right," I said, trying to get more. "Even if you can't confirm it. . . ."

Oppitz's mouth went into a set line. He was annoyed, all right.

"We thought he was contributing the Lamberti to the orchestra, that's true."

I thought I would fall off my chair. "What?"

He nodded, giving me a rather embittered smile. "There was every indication. He always brought it and played along with us and showed it to the string players."

"Was that all?"

No, no, said Oppitz. "No, he told me several times that he had a very big surprise for us, and he would wink. He told us that he hoped one day to hear one of our fine concertmasters playing the Lamberti."

"But he never came right out and told you?"

"Not directly. But he told Mrs. Hammerstein, and she told us."

"Mrs. Hammerstein?"

"A dear friend of his. She told us we were getting it, and that Mr. Lambert was looking forward to presenting it. How did you find this out? It was a very well-kept secret. And then—"

"And then you didn't get it?"

"Dennis was given the Scarampella." He let out a breath. "It's a very fine instrument. We're not complaining."

"I see." He could just about not stand it.

"If you write about the competition, Mr. Fitzgerald, I don't think you should mention the Stradivarius. Because, you know, it was never promised in so many words."

"Right. So what happened?"

"Well, when Dennis and I went to pick up the violin, it was a Stefano Scarampella."

"You expected it would be the Stradivarius?"

He nodded. "I guess we got the wrong idea."

"You went to Mr. Lambert's house, and he gave you the violin?"

"What? No, no. No, by that time Mr. Lambert had left us, you see."

"Jamison Lambert was dead?"

"Yes."

"Well, how did you get the Scarampella violin for Dennis Hanley?"

"We picked it up at Charles LaPorte's."

"LaPorte's?"

"Yes. He's a dealer in fine violins, you know. Mr. Lambert had told us to pick it up there."

"You went to LaPorte's expecting to get a Stradivarius and were given a different violin?" I said.

Oppitz nodded. "We were quite disappointed."

"Yes," I agreed. "But how did Jason Lambert get involved?"

"Oh, well, you see, Jamison was going to present it, but then he... So young Lambert came around to see us, and he agreed to make the presentation in his uncle's place."

"Mr. Oppitz, did Jason think you were getting the Stradivarius too?"

Oppitz reacted to that by crossing his arms and scratching both elbows at the same time.

"Now it's funny you should ask that," he said. "Because he came in here very upset, storming really, and demanded to see the violin his uncle was giving us. But when he looked at it, he didn't seem to mind."

"You mean he thought you were getting the Lamberti too?"

Oppitz frowned. "I don't know. I just don't know. I always thought something... unusual had happened."

21

SOMETIMES YOU HAVE to go backward to go forward. That's what I was doing, tracking Jamison Lambert's ghost along Central Park West.

You go north from Columbus Circle up along Central Park. The big old residence hotels have fronts on them like Masonic temples, and the apartments have eight big rooms. It's Woody Allen country. That's where Oppitz told me I would find Florence Hammerstein.

She had an apartment overlooking the park and had lived there since before World War II. A petite, soft-spoken woman who shopped at Zabar's, she looked as though she belonged on the *Normandie* crossing from Le Havre in the 1930s.

Florence Hammerstein let me in and insisted upon serving coffee and little cakes at a table in a sort of foyer. She was an aging wisp of a thing, with bright, lively gray eyes and a birdlike manner.

"I guess I knew Jamison as well as anyone," she told me shyly. "We were . . . keeping company, I guess you'd call it. Poor Jamison."

"Why do you say that?" I asked her. I was sipping very sweet, creamy coffee *mit Schlag* from a tiny china cup. It was something out of Vienna.

She looked toward the front of the apartment, toward the windows, beyond which was the park. "He was such a tentative person, Mr. Fitzgerald. He was always in a holding pattern, circling. He kept circling all his life, waiting to land. Or maybe to take off."

I watched the sparrowlike Florence and saw a young girl there, an eager but shy spirit perched at a window watching the busy world across the street in the park. I had the feeling she had never quite taken off, either.

"I'm trying to find out anything I can about a violin he owned. A Stradivarius."

Florence nodded her head knowingly. "Yes, yes. The Lamberti. Jamie used to play it constantly. He loved it so much. Even though it destroyed him."

I took out a Tiparillo and started to light it. Looking at my demure, aged hostess, I thought better of it and put it away again.

"The Stradivarius destroyed him?" I prompted her.

She smiled a faraway smile. "Well, you see, Mr. Fitzgerald, it was a curse. It's like being given a wish, and the thing you wish for is the worst thing that could happen."

There was Jamison, the excited, tentative son of the great violin virtuoso Gilberto Lamberti, growing up in a red plush box at Carnegie Hall, listening to his father dazzle the world. It was a glorious youth for the boy, crowned in a magnificent tenth birthday celebration at which he was presented with the gift of the Magi.

Flo Hammerstein had heard the story many times, she told me. It was a litany lovingly recalled by Jamison, an event set in marble in his mind: the gift of the Stradivarius.

Angelo Lamberti, a successful importer, had discovered to his joy that his son, Gilberto, was a prodigy and for his tenth birthday had given him a Stradivarius that would eventually be called the Lamberti. And when Gilberto's own son, Jamison, was ten years old, Gilberto had given him the violin.

"Gilberto continued to play it, you know, but it was understood that it would be Jamison's. It was to be a tradition, you see. Too bad his father didn't give him an air rifle," she sighed.

An air rifle? I had to smile at that. A bee-bee gun, we used to call them.

"Or a baseball bat," she continued. "He could never live up to it, you see. He was never much more than a passable amateur. And owning a Stradivarius..." She gave me a wan, ironic look.

"What happened?" I asked.

The birdlike head nodded thoughtfully. "What *could* happen? He tried. For years. And everyone pretended he was getting better. His father was Gilberto Lamberti, and he owned a Stradivarius, so he was expected to take his place in the world of music."

She blinked and turned away. "There are people of whom things are expected. And it's even worse if the person expects it of himself."

Such people, she said, can sometimes live a lifetime of expectancy without ever really *becoming* anything quite finished.

"So he worked at the shop, and everybody pretended he was a violinist."

"What shop?"

"The Gondolier. It was the family business. His grandfather founded it."

"Gilberto's father?"

"Yes. He was very successful. Everybody wanted something from Italy in those days."

"The Gondolier is still in business, isn't it?" I asked.

Flo Hammerstein tossed her head. "Oh, I think the nephew has a shop downtown, yes. But the real business is gone. Jamison just couldn't run it. He had no more talent at the import business than he had on the violin."

"What happened to the violin?" I asked her.

"More coffee?" she wanted to know, and poured without really noticing my response. *Mit Schlag*, of course.

"Thanks."

"Jamie never saw the violin as a curse. No, to him it was

139

a trust. Something to be passed on to someone who could measure up to it, as he hadn't."

"Mr. Oppitz, the orchestra manager, said he thought Jamison was going to give the violin to the youth orchestra," I told her.

"Yes, that's right," she said. "He wanted young geniuses to play it."

"Do you know why he changed his mind?"

She looked at me in surprise. "Change his mind? He didn't change his mind."

"He didn't?"

"Why, no. What makes you think that?"

"The winner, young Dennis Hanley, didn't receive the Lamberti," I told her.

"He didn't?" She cocked her head in confusion. "Well, that *is* odd! He was supposed to."

"You don't know what happened?"

Florence Hammerstein was bewildered. "No. He told me that's what he was going to do, and then... well, I didn't hear anymore. I just lost interest."

A lover's quarrel, I wondered, between these two tentative old friends?

"He never told you?" I tried again.

Her eyes were watery. "That's when he passed away, Mr. Fitzgerald. So, you see, I never heard anymore. I just couldn't go to that concert."

"Oh."

"If the orchestra boy didn't get the violin," she said, "who did?"

"His nephew."

She shot a dark look at me. "Jason? Oh, my."

"Why?"

"Jamie would have been very upset."

"He didn't like Jason?"

"Oh, no, Mr. Fitzgerald, not at all."

I walked back down Central Park West to 59th Street

and stood by the monument to the Spanish-American War and the blowing up of the battleship *Maine*. I lighted that Tiparillo that had been only tentative when I was with Florence Hammerstein and tried to think.

I was suddenly reminded of Watergate and the gap in the Nixon tapes. Because I kept coming up against a gap too: the Stradivarius gap.

The violin had been taken to LaPorte's apparently, and was supposed to have been claimed there by young Dennis Hanley. But he got a Scarampella instead.

What had happened to the Stradivarius at that point? Somehow it had found its way into Erik Halvorsen's hands and then back into the hands of Jason Lambert, Jamison's nephew.

And during that somehow time, two men had died.

I became more interested than ever in Jason Lambert and his shop in SoHo, the Gondolier.

I crossed to the Columbus Circle island NYP parking zone and started up the slanty blue Monte Carlo. *Arunga . . . runga . . . runga . . . .* Finally it spluttered to half-life. Then over to the West Side Highway and south downtown to Prince Street, and back into SoHo to the Gondolier.

The girl with the glasses in her hair smiled and chirped at me again and then went to whisper through the beaded curtain to Jason.

He looked out at me and seemed to shake his head a little in exasperation. Then he came out.

"You're that reporter again?"

"Yes, Mr. Lambert, I was wondering—"

"I don't understand what you want," he said irritably. "Detective Wilson said you're trying to make a big story out of this for some reason."

Good old Wilson.

"No bigger a story than it is," I said. "I understand your uncle planned to give his Stradivarius away in a violin competition."

"He what?"

"Yes. The Lamberti Competition. Do you know anything about that?"

"No, I don't," he snapped. "Those people were always after him for something."

"You mean, he didn't plan to give it to the competition?"

Jason Lambert's face went into a furious pout. "Are you crazy?" he said. "Give away a Stradivarius? Really!"

"Well, see, that's why I'm confused," I said, trying not to drive him into an angry silence. "It *sounded* crazy."

"Well. Now you know." He apparently was about to go back behind the beads.

I glanced at his helper. She was arranging glass figurines. They looked like gewgaws from Murano.

"Didn't your uncle take the violin to LaPorte's to be refurbished?" I asked.

"Yes, of course. You already know that, don't you?"

"And later you went and picked it up?"

"Why shouldn't I?" he said. "It was left to me in his will. I'm his only living relative."

"And you never heard anything about giving the violin to the competition?"

"Certainly not."

I stood there looking at the angry little three-piece-suit nephew and couldn't think of anything to say.

There were still some cadenzas missing from the Lamberti Sonata.

22

THAT NIGHT AT my place on East 82nd Street, after Ariel had left for "Les Miserables," I retreated to the bathtub with Marcus Aurelius and looked for solace from *Meditations*.

"The world is so enveloped in veils that it has seemed to many distinguished philosophers altogether unintelligible," Marcus told me.

Well, he was right about that, as usual.

"Enveloped in veils," indeed. Then and there I decided to drop the whole damn thing and let Detective Wilson take care of it. It was his job, after all. Maybe Wilson was right, anyway. Maybe Mitch Rogers would break and tell them where the gun was.

I allowed myself to think about Vermont and a life away from the craziness of the Big Apple.

"Fitzgerald, *Daily World*," I said, trying out my new job title.

There we would be, Ariel and I, skiing Mount Mansfield, lapping up Swiss fondue in front of a fire in Stowe. And I could start writing. I could write about New York, at last. God knows, you can't do it here, not while you're pounding out murders under the smoke signals of Ironhead Matthews.

Of course, I must have been sending up smoke signals of my own at the time, telling the world that Fitz was immersed in a comfortable cocoon of a tub and sailing away in reverie.

Because that's when the phone rang.

I slopped out of the tub to the phone, holding a towel around me.

"Yeah?"

"Fitz?" It was Rick Mazzili, the four-to-twelve man on the city desk at the *Daily Press*.

"What's up, Rick?"

"Listen, weren't you working on a story about a violin dealer?"

"What? What happened?"

Well, said Mazzili, a call had come in about a woman shot to death in front of Carnegie Hall.

"Danny beat it up there and got some photos, and he just called in. He said the woman came out of that guy LaPorte's place."

"Who is she?" I asked anxiously.

"That's why I called you. You want to hop over there?"

"Is that all you know?"

"That's it, kiddo. Danny's got pictures, but the cops are sitting on it at the moment. Since you did that story on LaPorte, I thought you might be able to clean it up for us."

"OK."

I threw on some clothes and hurried outside into a driving rain. Naturally, it has to be coming down in buckets when you get roused from a comfortable tub.

I drove across town to Carnegie Hall and saw the blue-and-whites angled in around the front of the marquee, the cops in slickers under the rain. I slid in next to them, got out, and walked over.

A crime scene had been established, with yellow lines around to keep people back. I ducked under the line and saw the lump on the sidewalk under the marquee, one part of a shoe sticking out.

A uniformed cop stopped me, and I got out my press card and hooked it into my coat lapel with a paper clip.

"*Daily Press*."

He nodded but still kept me from going any closer.

"Any I.D.?" I asked nervously.

"Nothing positive," he said. "Squad's on the way."

"Wilson?" I asked.

The cop gave me a look. "Yeah. You know anything about this?"

I lighted a Tiparillo and stared at the shapeless form under the blanket.

"Maybe," I said. "Can I take a look?"

"No way!" the uniformed cop said sternly.

"I might know who it is."

"Wilson will be here."

There was a flash, and I looked up to see Danny Malone still shooting photos. I walked over to him and drew him back under the yellow strip.

"Hey, Danny. What's this about her coming out of LaPorte's?"

Danny nodded his head toward the other side of 57th Street. "I was up here on the LaPorte story," he said. "That was your story, right? That's his place across the street there."

He drew me over to a woman standing against the wall of the building, trying to avoid the rain.

"She saw her."

I moved over to the woman, pale-faced under a hat with a little brim on it. She was blinking at me with curiosity as I came closer.

"Fitzgerald, *Daily Press*," I told her. "Did you see anything?"

She moved out from the building and pointed across 57th Street. "I was waiting for a bus across the street there," she said. "All the traffic started halting, and I saw she was running across right in front of the cars."

A man ran out into the street after her, she said. "I thought he was trying to help her. Then I saw he was chasing her."

"What else?"

"I couldn't see too well. They got across the street and the cars started again. Then when I looked again, I saw her down on the sidewalk."

"What about the man?"

"He was gone."

"Did you see where she came from?"

The woman moved out to the curb and pointed across the street. "That building there ... I think she came out the door."

"What makes you think that?" I asked her.

"Well, she was out into the street when I saw her, but the man came out through that door after her. So I think she came out ahead of him."

Then a squad car rolled up, and disgorged Detectives Wilson and Nickerson. Wilson huddled his shoulders against the rain and slipped in under the marquee. I hurried over, ducked under the yellow police line, and came up next to him.

He closed his eyes and rolled his head, about as happy to see me as if I were his ex-wife.

"What ... already?"

He and Nickerson walked over to the uniformed cop and stood there talking softly. The cop handed him a purse, and he shuffled some papers.

Then he moved to the body. I inched over closer. He lifted the blanket, and I experienced jangling emotions of sorrow and relief: relief that it wasn't Ariel; sorrow that it was Wilma Manning, LaPorte's secretary.

Wilson dropped the blanket, stepped back, and bumped into me.

"Well," he said sourly, "did you get a look?"

I nodded.

"Shit," he muttered.

I walked up to the corner in the rain and called the city desk to give them a brief fill-in on what I had up till then. Then it was back to the crime scene to stand around and wait.

The forensics squad and an Assistant Medical Examiner went over the body and the scene pretty thoroughly, and Wilson and Nickerson talked to people, including the woman in the hat.

Then the two cops went across 57th Street and into the building where LaPorte had had his office. I followed. We rode up in the elevator and found the door to LaPorte's unlocked.

Inside, in LaPorte's office, a light was still on. There were New York State Lottery tickets lying on his desk, with a rubber band beside them.

"She must have been here, working late," he said. "Then she went out and somebody got her."

"Who?" I asked.

"Yeah."

I had to leave to phone in the rest of what I had. Naturally, I couldn't touch any phone in LaPorte's, so it was back down in the elevator again, outside into the rain, and up to the phone booth on the corner.

From there, I could see the half-round canvas canopy over the entrance to LaPorte's building. Wilma Manning had come out under that canopy and dashed out into moving traffic, pursued by someone who shot her under the marquee of Carnegie Hall.

I could just hear Wilson's explanation. "A mugger spotting an easy mark ... a woman alone in the rain ... committing a crime of opportunity."

But I knew that wasn't it, and so did Wilson.

I wondered if whoever it was had finally found what he was looking for.

23

THERE'S NOTHING MORE frustrating for a newspaperman than to write something he knows isn't true, but that can't be helped. Usually it's a vauntful statement from some city councilman or drug enforcement officer to the effect that they're going to clean up the druggie mess in Bryant Park, or maybe that they've already cleaned it up. Then you walk by the New York Public Library and see the druggies doing business as usual.

I remember the police commissioner who became so incensed about "distorted" stories of crime in Central Park that he announced he was not afraid to walk right through at midnight. And he did. Oddly enough, the police commissioner of the City of New York was not mugged. This proved there was no crime there. The fact that stalwarts from the commissioner's squad were lurking behind every shrub and probably in the Central Park Zoo as well, disguised as gorillas, was beside the point.

Well, that's the kind of story I had to write about Wilma Manning. Some burglar had seen a light in LaPorte's office after business hours, Detective Wilson announced. He had gone in and robbed her, and when she fled he chased her outside and shot her.

You might think Manning's murder would cast doubt on his case against Mitch Rogers. But no. It simply proved there was no connection, Wilson explained.

Nothing had changed. Only Wilma Manning was dead. And this time I couldn't get him to tell me what ballistics had found. If it were a .25 caliber slug, it proved nothing in a city where handguns of all kinds exist in deadly profusion.

I was only thankful that Ariel was living with me and, I hoped, out of harm's way. I had never told her that somebody had taken some shots at me, and I hoped that whoever it was didn't know where I lived.

Ariel's future had become fixed upon Vermont and Allen State College. She couldn't wait to get out of New York. I couldn't blame her. I had promised I'd be ready as soon as the Erik Halvorsen murder was wrapped up, but now I was ready to go.

I called Terry Oakley, up in Vermont, and told him I'd like to talk about a job.

"Hey, that's great," he said over the phone.

Then he started haggling. I would have to undergo a try-out period, of course, he said with a little cough.

Try out? The dreadnought of the *Daily Press* trying out in Allen, Vermont?

Well, I told him, that was all right.

Ariel and I celebrated by going down to Foley Square for dinner at Giambone's. I invited Harry Reeves, who had a couple of bombs and then told me I was undergoing canyon fever.'

"What?"

"You walk around between all the stone buildings and they shut out the sun and your brain gets shaded," he said, his florid face bobbing around like Tip O'Neill's.

"What's he saying?" asked Ariel.

"It takes a while," I told her. "He has to pretend he's Mike Royko first."

"Yes," Harry went on, "you get shade poisoning, and that leads to canyon fever. Then you go get a job on the *East Jesus Gazette*, in the middle of God's country somewhere, and write about the Elks Club parade. When a decent murder comes along and the editor says he doesn't want that kind of news, you punch him out. Then you crawl back to the *Daily Press* on your belly."

Reeves reared back and guffawed.

Ariel gave me a less than pleased glance.

I sipped on Schaefer and puffed my Tiparillo.

I didn't entirely give up on the Halvorsen case. In the few weeks before we would be leaving, I went around to see Hendrik Van Leeb and gave him my card and told him what I wanted. He said he'd let me know.

When I told Ironhead Matthews I was quitting the *Daily Press* to go to Vermont, he looked at me as though I had announced I was signing myself into Bellevue.

"Vermont?" he said, loading the word with spittle and revulsion.

He suggested I take a vacation.

The *Daily Press* gang tossed me a going-away party at Costello's that is still discussed as one of the most disgraceful episodes in New York journalism.

Bike O'Malley was persuaded to try Brandy Alexanders and then told Ironhead Matthews exactly what he thought of him. Several times. Ironhead fired him.

Jim Owens insisted he had only accidentally gotten his hand caught in Peggy the waitress's apron and did not deserve what Big Jim the bartender did to him.

Jerry Schlamp drew an immense cartoon of me chasing a goddam cow through Vermont trying to interview it.

Ariel huddled in a corner and said that if she had known what newspapermen were really like, she would have gotten off the elevator the first time she saw me.

It was glorious.

I awakened the next day inside a keg of hardened cement. From somewhere, the Allen, Vermont, Elks Club Marching Band was tromping through my brain playing tubas and bass drums. They were marching thunderously down Wall Street, so that every *whump* and *booboop* bounced off the canyon walls and slammed back inside my poor head.

Then some idiot went to work with a glockenspiel,

plinking little bell sounds that penetrated my ear.

I got up somehow and staggered to the phone.

"Yeah."

"Fitzgerald?"

"I think so."

"What? Is that you, Mr. Fitzgerald?"

I finally admitted it.

"Van Leeb," he said. "What do you think I have here in front of me?"

I was in no mood for guessing games. I knew what I had in front of me. Total destruction.

"What?" I said.

"What you wanted."

I felt as though I would explode. "Terrific."

It was the way I had thought, he went on. He had dutifully perused each catalogue that came in from Sotheby's and Christie's and the other auction houses, and today he had found it.

"Linton's Auction House," he said pregnantly.

"What about it?"

An edge of annoyance slid into Van Leeb's voice. Had he been checking these catalogues for me for no reason? Was I interested or not?

I sat down, and gradually it came through.

"No, I'm very interested," I managed to say. "Linton's you say? When?"

"This afternoon."

Today? Oh, Jupiter Optimus Maximus! Why did it have to be today?

"You just got it and it's today?" I muttered.

Van Leeb admitted the catalogue had come in earlier, but that he hadn't had time to read it. He had checked Sotheby's and Christie's catalogues religiously, but Linton's was a smaller house and not a top priority.

"Okay," I said. "Thanks. Can you be there?"

"I wouldn't miss it."

24

LINTON'S AUCTION HOUSE is on Third Avenue in the sixties, and like Sotheby's and Christie's it's a big barn of a place with showrooms filled with statuary, paintings, rare books, and gilt-covered cupids from English mansions and French châteaux.

"A *what* . . . an *auction*?" Ariel complained when she woke up and saw me dressing to go out.

"Stay in bed," I told her. "You don't have to get up yet."

But she shook her head and got up too. She said she had always wanted to go to an auction, and maybe we could find something for Vermont.

"I never thought you'd get up early on a Saturday to go to an auction." She smiled

"It's not that early," I reminded her. But I didn't tell her why I was going.

Anyway, we got dressed and she had some coffee. I had Alka-Seltzer and a Pepsi, which she considered weird.

"It's the only thing that stops the Elks Club Band," I explained. She thought that was even weirder.

I was unaware of any NYP parking zones near Linton's so we rode over in a taxi. By then, Ariel was sitting up and taking notice and wondering what in the world I wanted to buy.

"A violin."

She gave me a blank look. "You're not taking up music, I hope."

We jumped out of the cab in front of Linton's and hurried inside into a pretty crowded Saturday-afternoon auction. I picked up a catalogue from a stack on the counter just inside the front door and went to sit in a chair to look it over.

Ariel had one too, and she was also reading it.

Everything was for sale, including the art collection of the late wife of an Italian count: paintings, jewelry, crystal. But I didn't see what I was looking for.

I hurried back to the counter by the front door, where two women were checking lists and making notes.

"Is this everything?" I asked.

One of the women looked up inquiringly. "What? Oh! No, there are a couple of added starters." She reached under the counter and brought out another slim brochure.

I opened it, and there it was, in living color.

Item 284: Stradivarius. The Lamberti. Authenticated with complete iconography. Floor bid: $250,000.

Ariel was beside me looking over my shoulder.

"My God, is that it?"

I nodded and led her back to the folding chairs that had been set up in the main auction room. In front of an upraised platform behind a lectern stood the auctioneer, already going down the list.

Ariel was all atwitter beside me, poring over the little brochure.

"How did you know?" she asked. "Who's selling it?"

It was a good question. I looked over the brochure. The seller was listed as "Anonymous."

I was on my feet again. The auctioneer had just knocked down a Tiffany lamp when I reached him.

"Say"—I waved at him—"can I get a look at Item Two Eighty-Four?"

The auctioneer leaned down to me. "What?"

"I'd like to have a look at one of the items. The Stradivari violin."

The auctioneer was sweating, his face flushed. "Oh, well ... uh ... I think it's in the Trianon Gallery."

153

"Where?"

"That room to the left."

People were milling around in the aisles, waiting for the next item. I pushed through them to the Trianon Gallery and inside. A large showroom, it was jammed with objets d'art; also a large man and a slim woman wearing a robin's-egg-blue suit.

"Yes?"

"I want to have a look at the Lamberti," I told the blue-suited woman.

"But that was earlier," she said.

"What was?"

"The examination period. The last three days."

"I didn't know. Can I look at it now?"

Oh, my. Well, that was quite out of the question, she said, glancing at the large man beside her. "There was ample time during the examination period," she explained smoothly.

"But I have to look at it," I said.

"Are you bidding on it?"

I dodged that question. Not with a floor bid of $250,000.

"It isn't that," I said.

Linton's Auction House had rules, she said. Just because it wasn't as well known yet as Sotheby's didn't mean that it was not operated in a professional manner. Linton's had a growing reputation.

"Well, can you tell me who the seller is?" I asked.

Blue Suit checked her clipboard. "The seller has requested anonymity."

"You mean, nobody can find out who it is?"

Of course somebody could find out, she said. The person who bought the Stradivarius would know and be fully satisfied in all particulars. But not just anybody.

Somebody was hissing. I glanced around. Ariel was standing in the doorway waving at me. "The violin... they're selling it."

I left Blue Suit and her bodyguard and hurried back into the large auction room. The flushed auctioneer was going through a lush description of the grand Lamberti. "Once played with incomparable brilliance by the virtuoso Gilberto Lamberti..."

Then I saw the large impresario form pushing through the bidders, and Hendrik Van Leeb slid into a folding chair beside me.

"There you are," I said. "Are you going to bid on it?"

Van Leeb took out a little pad and a golden pen. "Of course," he whispered.

Ariel was tugging at my elbow. "That's Van Leeb," she whispered. "He's a famous dealer."

"I know. I told him to be here."

She looked at me. "*You* told him...?"

But there was no time for any more, because the auctioneer was finishing his spiel.

"...offered by an anonymous seller with full authentication."

Then I noticed the auctioneer spot Van Leeb and nod a professional welcome.

I did a quick survey of the crowd, looking for the face of Jason Lambert. He was toward the back, standing at the edge of the crowd, his eyes fixed on the auctioneer.

And then the bidding was under way.

Right away, somebody said "Two fifty," and somebody else went twenty-five more, and then Van Leeb said "Three hundred."

I realized he meant $300,000.

I glanced at Jason. He was barely able to contain his joy.

Another bid put the price to three fifty.

Then there was a pause. I looked at Van Leeb. He shook his head no.

"Three fifty once," said the auctioneer.

"Don't you want it?" I poked Van Leeb.

"Not that much."

"Going twice for three fifty," said the auctioneer. "Surely there are music lovers here?"

"Four hundred," somebody yelled, and I thought Ariel Ryan was going to faint, because the bidder was me.

Something crashed into my ribs. "Fitz!"

An elegant man in a pearl-gray suit across the aisle from me shot a scornful look in my direction. He seemed confused when he saw Hendrik Van Leeb. Possibly Van Leeb wasn't dropping out?

The pearl-gray gentleman said "Four five."

"Four fifty!" I declared.

Ariel kicked me. I glanced at Van Leeb. An amused smile was on his face. He crossed his legs.

The pearl-gray gentleman knew by now it wasn't Van Leeb who was dueling with him, but some unknown gallant who hardly looked the part.

I noticed the robin's-egg-blue suit sliding down the aisle past me, turning to glance at this hopeful bidder. She saw Van Leeb beside me and kept going. I saw her give a sort of body-language shrug to the auctioneer.

"Five," said the pearl-gray suit.

"Six!" From somebody who couldn't afford to get his car fixed. Van Leeb's body was trembling slightly.

"Six?" said the auctioneer, studying the pearl-gray suit. That worthy was looking dead ahead now, unwilling to peek in my direction.

"Going once for six hundred thousand," said the smiling auctioneer. "Do I hear any other bids?"

He surveyed the crowd.

"Going twice," he said. And then, "Sold!"

And Ariel covered her face with her hands.

25

"Come on," I told Van Leeb.

I got up and hurried back down the aisle into the Trianon Gallery, followed by Van Leeb.

The little robin met me there, smiling and examining my face with a certain curiosity. Then she turned her attention to the great violin dealer.

"You won't be sorry," she cooed to him.

Van Leeb only smiled. "Not me. This gentleman."

Another look at me. Doubt crowded out curiosity.

"You?" she murmured, examining me critically. "But .. we assumed he was with you." Then, to me, "Sir, are you sure you're a responsible bidder?"

"Absolutely," I said. "If this is what it purports to be."

"Why, sir!"

"May I see the violin?"

Reluctantly, it seemed to me, she walked into a little side room and came out with a violin case. She put it on a glass countertop and opened it.

I looked at the beautiful orange thing and motioned Van Leeb to come closer. He slid over next to me.

"Well?"

Van Leeb lifted the violin with professional gentleness and examined it with his eyes, all the while nodding in satisfaction.

"Yes ... yes ... unmistakable ... Here, look."

He held the violin up for me to look through the left "f hole" into the interior at a slip of paper glued to the back inside.

Antonius Stradivarius Cremonensis
Faciebat Anno 1722

There was also Stradivari's unique trademark, a double circle containing a cross and the initials *A.S.*

The little auctioneer lady was beside me again. "How did you say you will be paying?" she insisted.

I lifted the violin bow from the case and handed it to Van Leeb.

"Have a look."

Van Leeb looked at the bow for a second and frowned.

"Is this the bow?" he asked.

The blue lady was between us. "Yes, of course."

Hendrik Van Leeb issued a scornful grunt. "This is a fake."

I thought the lady in blue was going to faint. "What?" she gasped. "Mr. Van Leeb!"

"What's the matter with it?" I jumped in.

Van Leeb stood there shaking his head. "I'm sorry, but this bow was not made by Antonio Stradivari."

"But we have authentication," said the lady, her eyes narrowing.

"May we see it?" I demanded imperiously. Or at least as imperiously as is possible for an ink-stained wretch.

"Well ..." She appealed to Van Leeb.

"Mr. Van Leeb is here as my expert," I said commandingly. "If he authenticates the violin *and* the bow, I'm prepared to pay."

I glanced at Ariel, whose white face and fixed eyes seemed to be asking, With what, for God's sake!

Well, the lady in the blue suit hurried away and returned a few minutes later with a large manila envelope. She opened the clasp and slid the certificate out onto the counter.

But before I could pick it up, here came somebody marching into the Trianon Gallery like Foreign Minister Joachim von Ribbentrop of the Third Reich calling on the foreign minister of Poland.

Jason Lambert. Steaming.

"What is going on here?" he demanded Napoleonically.

"Hello, Jason."

Jason quickly glared at everybody, from Van Leeb to Ariel to me.

The lady in blue shuffled her feet. "Uh, Mr. Lambert . . . this gentleman put in the top bid, and—"

"What?" Jason looked fire at me. "Miss Simmons, are you crazy!"

Miss Simmons's face went beet red. This was all too distressing.

"I really don't know what to do," she said in a flutter.

I picked up the violin bow. "This bow wasn't made by Stradivari," I told him.

Jason sneered. "And how would anybody like *you* know that?"

I indicated my expert. "Do you know Hendrik Van Leeb?"

Jason bristled and his mouth went into a tight line. "I haven't had the pleasure."

"Mr. Van Leeb is an eminent luthier. Mr. Van Leeb just told me this bow can be bought at Woolworth's for a dollar-three-eighty," I said.

Jason swayed a little, but he stood his ground. "I don't care what he says. The papers guarantee it."

Ah, yes, the certificate. I picked it up from the counter and looked it over, motioning Van Leeb closer to look as well.

The certificate stated that the violin was the Lamberti, all right, and listed the owners from Count Brugen all the way down to Jason Lambert.

It was of recent issue, on the letterhead stationery of Charles LaPorte, luthier, and began: *I certify that the violin in the possession of Jason Lambert is in my opinion a work of Antonio Stradivari of Cremona and bears his label dated 1722.*

"This is new," I said. "When was this made out?"

"When I took possession, of course," snapped Jason.

"Why did you need a new one?" I pressed him. "Why wasn't the original certificate signed over to you?"

"I wouldn't know," he said angrily. "I suppose when a violin changes hands, a new certificate is issued."

I looked at the certificate, signed at the bottom "Charles LaPorte" in a scrawl that could have been anybody's writing. And neither LaPorte nor Wilma Manning were around to challenge that signature.

Suddenly I realized why a new certificate was necessary. The original paper must have signed the Lamberti over to the Metropolitan Youth Symphony Orchestra.

"Where's the original?"

Jason said impatiently that he knew of no other papers than these.

"Mr. Van Leeb," he said, "if you're the expert you say you are, is this an authentic certificate?"

"It is," agreed Van Leeb.

"But what do you have to show the violin was given to you?" I pressed on.

"I have my uncle's will," said Jason heatedly. "And it allows me to sell this violin."

"I believe it's all quite satisfactory," said Miss Simmons over my shoulder.

Jason smiled.

"If you're buying, I want the money," he declared. "If you're not a responsible bidder, I want the violin taken back out to be offered again."

"I really think—" Miss Simmons started.

I cut her off. "I tell you what. Let's get Detective Wilson up here. I want to know if this bow you're offering as a Stradivari is bogus."

"Why don't you go to hell!"

"Because, Jason," I told him, "I know who has the real

bow. Because when you shot Erik Halvorsen, he had already sold the bow, and—"

That's as far as I got. One deft hand snatched the Lamberti, the other grabbed the certificate, and Jason Lambert darted between the glass counters and out of the Trianon Gallery.

I went after him, but I couldn't get past the big bodyguard, who also set off in pursuit, moving pretty fast, at that, for a big man.

Jason burst out of the gallery into the main room just as workmen were jockeying a great landscape painting through toward the auctioneer. It was about ten feet wide and eight feet high with windmills in the distance and a lovely lake in the center.

Jason went right through the lake.

I went through behind him.

I could hear howls of outrage behind me as I got to the front door and saw Jason sprinting toward Third Avenue and into the northbound traffic.

Honking and cursing, and then Jason dodged a car, clunked onto the hood of another, and went sprawling. Ahead of him, the Lamberti went skittering across the street under the traffic.

26

I WISH I could say that my brilliant ploy at Linton's Auction House broke everything wide open and won me what Mike Santangelo the rewrite man calls "the Putzala prize." I wish I could say that Detective Toupee Wilson and Ironhead Matthews were thrilled and heaped praise upon me for my initiative. I especially wish I could say that I treed Jason Lambert like a possum.

But the unhappy facts are that when Wilson came screaming up Third Avenue in a squad car with a little light on the roof and jumped out of the car, all anybody wanted to talk about was the priceless Stradivarius that had gone under a Transit Authority bus and the Neanderthal pillaging of *Lake Windmills*, which somebody had desecrated like Alaric the Ostrogoth.

Traffic was at a standstill on Third Avenue in front of the auction house, which caused enough violent honking and vrooming and exhaust fumes to attract a cloud of traffic cops. The large bodyguard from Linton's stood in the street holding back the bus, and who but Miss Simmons of the robin's-egg-blue suit went squirming underneath it to retrieve the violin.

I had one arm on Jason's chicken neck, and the other one holding his right arm behind his back.

Hendrik Van Leeb stood on the curb in front of Linton's, shaking, and I couldn't tell from what. Ariel still had a hand over her mouth, but her eyes were as large as 150-watt bulbs.

Everybody wanted to know everything at the same time,

and everybody also wanted to tell everybody everything at the same time.

Naturally, when Detective Wilson jumped out, he was the one everybody zeroed in on.

"Make this maniac take his hands off me!" shrieked Jason.

"... ran right through the painting..."

"... scratched, gouged, and pummeled..."

"... not even a responsible bidder..."

"... suits will be filed promptly..."

"... totally unacceptable..."

Well, the auction-house people, Jason, and I all wound up in the squad room at the West 10th Street station house, where a red-faced and scowling Wilson looked us all over and put his thumb and a fingertip on his closed eyelids.

Right away, Miss Simmons and her hulking fullback wanted me arrested for destroying *Lake Windmills*, and then, when they heard I was a reporter, they swore they would sue the *Daily Press* for the commission they were due.

I explained I only followed Jason through the gaping hole he had made and was an innocent bystander.

Then Simmons held up the Stradivarius and showed scratches and scrapes on it, and I thought she was going to swoon.

I would be sued for that too.

Finally, Wilson took his fingertips off his eyelids and told Simmons and the fullback that the painting and the violin were "not my headache" and sent them downstairs to tell their troubles to the desk sergeant.

"And leave the violin here," he finished.

They left, cackling like hens.

Jason sat there like a puffed-up little frog and demanded to know why he had been brought in.

Wilson glared at me, possibly thinking the same thing.

"Investigation," he finally said uncertainly.

"Of what?"

Wilson sat at his desk and started drawing targets.

"Why did you run out of Linton's?" I asked, trying to be helpful.

"I thought you were trying to steal my violin," proclaimed the impudent little main-chancer.

Wilson frowned at me. And drew a little circle. Then he looked at Jason. Another circle. Then he threw his pen aside.

"How did Fred Cerutti get that bow?" I asked Jason.

"How would I know?" he came right back.

"Who's Fred Cerutti?" Detective Wilson interjected, and I realized I had given up the name of a confidential source. But it couldn't be helped now.

"A Queens businessman," I said. "Erik Halvorsen sold him the bow that goes with this violin." I turned back to Jason. "Erik had your violin."

Little red splotches colored Jason's cheeks. I had him in a hammerlock now.

"How do you explain that?"

"I don't have to explain anything," he said. "What La-Porte did when he had the violin, I don't know. If he or this Halvorsen sold the bow, I want it back."

Wilson did an eye roll. Instead of solving things for him, I was complicating them. My hammerlock hold slipped a little. I tried again.

"You killed Erik to get the violin back," I told him. "But you didn't know the bow had already been sold."

Jason took in a big breath. "Will you listen to this?" he muttered. "I got the violin from LaPorte. This officer was there, and so were you."

I glanced at Wilson's yellow pad. He was making exclamation points and stars.

Jason dug into his wallet, pulled out a folded smudged paper, and tossed it on the desk in front of Wilson.

"There! That's a copy of my uncle's will. Everything is left to me."

Wilson picked it up and scanned it with a face that grew more disgusted with each sentence. He handed it back to Jason.

"Yes." He sighed. "It seems to be in order."

Jason grabbed the paper back and stuffed it into his wallet. He was standing there quivering with rage.

"Officer, am I under arrest?" he asked snippily.

"No."

"Is the Lamberti my property?"

"Yes, sir."

"Is there any reason why I can't sell my own property?"

"No, Mr. Lambert."

Jason darted a smoldering glance at me. "I will not be harassed by this ... this *vulture*," he boiled. "I want your assurance that he will leave me alone! All he wants is a phony story for that phony rag he works for."

Wilson let out a long breath. "He won't harass you any more."

And Jason sailed out with the Lamberti, the certificate, his uncle's will, and the assurance that I could no longer touch him.

27

"THIS IS THE last warning I'm giving you," Detective Wilson told me levelly.

"But, Wilson, he killed Erik! I'm sure of it."

Wilson seemed less than thunderstruck. He got up, walked to a hot plate, and poured himself some coffee in a yellow mug. Then he came back and sat down.

"How?" He sipped.

"Now, listen. Jamison Lambert gave that Stradivarius to the Metropolitan Youth Symphony Orchestra, see? Or at least, he tried to. But then he died, and Jason decided he wanted to keep it."

"Brilliant," said Wilson sarcastically. "Says who?"

"Says I," I said. "Now, something happened then, and I admit I'm not sure what."

"You admit to a screw-up? Only one?"

"Now, wait." I was trying to figure it out as I went along.

Jason must have gone to the orchestra to reclaim the Stradivarius and then discovered the one they were getting was not the Lamberti after all.

"So, he goes to LaPorte," I went on. "But LaPorte hasn't got the Lamberti either. He's given it to Erik Halvorsen to sell."

And then I had it.

"Wilson, that's it," I said, getting excited. "When Jamison Lambert died, LaPorte figured he had a priceless violin in his hands and nobody to claim it. That's why he tried to sell it through Erik, on the sly, rather than at a public auction. LaPorte knew the gift of the Lamberti was a secret, so he switched violins and gave them a different one."

Wilson was listening. Possibly he realized he might as well, since nothing would shut me up.

"Then what?" he asked.

"Well," I went on unsteadily, "Jason must have gone to see Erik to get the Stradivarius, but Erik wouldn't give it to him. So he shot him and took it."

Wilson was wagging his head.

"Wonderful," he said. "Except that Lambert left the violin to his nephew in his will. And we both saw him reclaim it from LaPorte's."

He sipped more coffee.

I lighted a Tiparillo and let out a cloud of smoke, trying to hide inside it.

I felt I had the truth fleetingly by the tail, but my grip was slipping. LaPorte must have destroyed the original papers and made out new ones so he could sell the Lamberti. But how did those papers get made out to Jason, and how did Jason reclaim the violin in front of our eyes?

I blew out more smoke to cover my exit.

That might have finally been the end of the case for me, if I hadn't happened to be at Ariel's place one afternoon as she gave a lesson to Dennis Hanley, the gifted Queens violinist who was going to be concertmaster for the final Metropolitan Youth Symphony Orchestra concert of the season at Carnegie Hall in November.

He was a tall, shy kid with wonderful slim hands, and he went at his violin playing with a lot of driving energy, like a halfback darting through a field of tacklers.

I asked him about Jamison Lambert.

"He was really a nice guy," Dennis said. "He told me he was looking forward to hearing me play the Lamberti."

"So you think he was going to give it to the orchestra?"

"I know it. He told me so."

I looked at him. "In so many words?"

"Sure."

"Did you tell that to Mr. Oppitz?" I asked.

"Heck, yes, I told him. But he said it would just cause trouble. I was going to ask Mr. Lambert about it, you know, at the concert."

"Which concert?"

"The concert when he was going to present the fiddle. But he didn't make it. He died just before."

Dennis went back to practicing under the stern eye of Ariel, and I sat there stewing about it all.

And then I realized something that had been under my nose all along, but that I hadn't considered. There was Jamison Lambert about to give away a priceless Stradivarius that was coveted by his nephew.

Jamison took the violin to LaPorte to be shined up in preparation for his wonderful surprise. And then, just before he was to give it away, he died, and the instrument reverted to Jason.

Jamison Lambert had died at a convenient moment.

Too convenient.

28

IT TOOK SOME cajoling and digging at the West 82nd Street station to find the report of the death of Jamison Lambert, but I finally got it. It sent me back down into SoHo to the Gondolier on Prince Street.

I sat in my blue clunker and smoked a Tiparillo until I saw Jason come out and walk up the street. Then I walked into the Gondolier to the lady with the glasses in her hair.

"Hi," I told her. "Fitzgerald, *Daily Press*. Have you heard from the police yet?"

The lady with the glasses blinked. "What?"

"Are you Julie Myers?" I asked with a stern look.

"Yes," she said, and stepped back a little.

"Then you're the one who found Jamison Lambert's body," I told her, and took out a reporter's pad to make notes.

Julie Myers pulled her glasses out of her hair and put them over her eyes. She stared at me wide-eyed.

"I don't understand," she said blankly.

"How did you happen to find the body?" I went on, trying not to give her time to think.

"Why... he didn't answer his phone," she said in a rush. "So Jason asked me to go to his apartment. Why?"

"Jason sent you to his uncle's apartment?"

"Yes. Because he kept calling and—"

"Had you ever been there before?" I went on.

"No," she said.

"How did you get in?"

"He gave me a key."

I stood there and tried to picture it. Julie Myers opens the door and goes in and finds Jamison dead.

"Where was he?"

"In bed."

"Do you know how he died?"

No, said Julie, he was simply dead. "I guess he died in his sleep."

"Was he ill or anything?"

She had no idea, she said. She had immediately called Jason, and then he and the police came, and that was all she knew.

Did she know anything about the Lamberti violin?

Julie knew that Jason's uncle was going to give it to an orchestra, and that Jason was furious about it.

"Did they quarrel about it?"

"Oh, yes! When Mr. Lambert came to the shop—he worked around here sometimes—they screamed at each other. Actually, Jason screamed, and Mr. Lambert wouldn't answer."

"What did Jason say, do you remember?"

"Well, he didn't want Mr. Lambert to change his will."

That hit me between the eyes. "Lambert was going to change his will?"

"Well, yes, to leave the violin to the orchestra."

"I see. But then he died?"

"Yes."

"And Jason sent you to find the body?"

Julie Myers blinked, and shoved her glasses back up into her hair.

"Well . . ."

Then I heard a soft tinkle, and saw Julie looking over my shoulder. I turned around, and there was Jason just inside the door, his face set in an expression of ice.

"Did you hear what that policeman said?" he snapped at me.

"Yes, I did."

"Julie," he flung out, "call the police."

Julie was frozen in her tracks, however. "Jason, he says the police are already on the way."

"What?" said Jason, moving toward me.

"Yes," I told him. "It's all over. They know."

Those red splotches colored Jason's cheeks again. "They know *what*?"

"They dug up your uncle's body, Jason. They know you killed him."

A gasp escaped from Julie Myers.

And a little white handgun appeared in Jason's hand.

"You son of a bitch," he spat out.

And I was down behind a counter with statues on it. *"Blam!"* A Venetian doge lost his head.

Julie was yelling and crawling on the floor. "Jason... for God's sake... what are you doing?"

"What did you tell him, you damned fool?" Jason screamed.

I crawled to the end of the counter and peeked around the side near the floor. Jason was crouched near the front door, holding his little gun. A .25 caliber, I had no doubt.

I remembered Erik' bloody chest on West 11th Street, and the shots that exploded glass panes behind my head on West 40th Street.

"Give it up!" I yelled. Another shot crashed into a Murano glass vase.

I heard scurrying and Julie Myers scrambled around behind the other end of the counter. She looked at me in wild fright.

"Throw something," I hissed at her.

"What?" She was a statue balled up on the floor.

"If he kills me, he'll kill you too."

That seemed to shock her into paying attention.

"Throw something," I repeated.

She reached around into a shelf, and was looking for something, and then she had it. She held it out for me to see.

The Lamberti.

I nodded. "Throw it as hard as you can toward the front window," I hissed at her.

"Oh, God," she muttered, and then let fly with the Stradivarius in a high arc up over the cases across the shop.

I peeked around the corner near the floor again and watched Jason as his priceless heirloom came sailing up over the brass lamps and Italian figurines.

Jason froze for a moment, his eyes fixed on the soaring fiddle. Then he reached up to catch it with both hands.

And I was around the counter and heading into him, gun, fiddle, and all. We went down in a scramble and crashed under a table over which a Venetian silk cloth was draped.

Jason was howling, under the green silk, and waving the gun around, trying to get off a shot. I aimed for the middle of the silk with everything I could put into it. The punch must have landed right in the center of his face, because the silk tablecloth slumped to the floor in a lump.

I pulled off the tablecloth. Jason was out cold. He was still holding the Lamberti.

29

IN THE END, they didn't have to dig up Jamison's body, because they had something else: the .25-caliber gun Jason had tried to export me with.

The little handgun—which had belonged to Uncle Jamison, by the way—told a story that could have been set to music: a funeral dirge.

It had fired the six shots that killed Erik Halvorsen, and the slugs that got Charles LaPorte and Wilma Manning as well. I have no doubt the bullets that exploded those panes of glass in the parking garage came from the gun too, but the cops never recovered enough of them to put through ballistics.

By the time Detectives Wilson and Nickerson got to the Gondolier, summoned by a phone call from the semi-hysterical Julie Myers, I was holding the gun and Jason was still sulking under the silk-covered table.

Sometimes when a guy figures he's caught, he's willing to tell you everything to show you how smart he is and how marvelous his plan was. The fact that it didn't work is beside the point. That's the way it was with Jason when we all wound up once more back in the West 10th Street squad room.

It had happened more or less as I had figured. There was Jason waiting for his uncle to die so he could get his brownstone and his Stradivarius, when the old fool announced he was going to give the violin away to some crazy orchestra.

The silly old man had expected Jason to be pleased with

the idea and had told him he was changing his will. Jason would still get the brownstone and the Gondolier, and that should certainly satisfy him. Uncle Jamison discovered how satisfied Jason was when a pillow came down over his face, and after that he didn't care anymore.

Jason had tricked Julie into "discovering" the body and then went to reclaim the Lamberti. That's when he discovered he wasn't the only person who had plans for the violin.

"LaPorte refused to give it to me," Jason said indignantly. "He said he had made out a new certificate giving it to the orchestra, and it was signed by my uncle."

But then Jason learned that the orchestra had been given a Scarampella. "I realized LaPorte was pulling a fast one."

When he went back to LaPorte, the excitable luthier had collapsed and admitted he was a crook, said Jason smugly.

"I threatened to turn him over to the police," said Jason, "and he started blubbering that he needed money to save his business and all that bullshit."

"Why didn't you go to the police?" said Wilson. "You had your uncle's will leaving it to you."

Jason made a face. He couldn't do that, he said, because he couldn't let the cops look into how his uncle had died.

"I didn't know you could tell he was smothered with a pillow by digging him up," Jason pouted.

I glanced at Detective Wilson, who had the good sense to say nothing.

Besides, there was the problem of that damned certificate giving the violin to the orchestra, he said. LaPorte admitted he had given the instrument to Erik with a certificate to sell it for him.

Jason had tracked down Erik and found him drunk and obnoxious and unwilling to believe that the violin belonged to Jason. "He said he had the papers, and it was

LaPorte's, and he had a deal going. Then he tried to tell me there was enough for all of us," Jason muttered.

The little white gun ended that conversation.

After that, Jason said mournfully, things got out of hand. He couldn't find the damned certificate at Erik's, and when he contacted Linton's to sell it, he was told he had to have the papers.

Then LaPorte, the idiot, tried to blackmail him, he said. "He told me if I had the violin, then I must have gotten Erik, and he told me a reporter was snooping around."

A look at me.

Anyway, Jason went to LaPorte and demanded the certificate. LaPorte tried to bargain with him. After all, he told Jason, the Lamberti didn't belong to either of them. LaPorte would provide papers if Jason would split with him. The little gun ended that conversation too, and Jason turned LaPorte's office upside down searching for the papers without success.

The same day he shot LaPorte, he drove down to the *Daily Press* and tried to remove me as well.

And still he didn't have the certificate. A search of Ariel Ryan's apartment didn't produce it, either.

Jason had a big problem. He had the violin but no papers, and if the original certificate surfaced giving it to the orchestra, he was finished.

Then one day Wilma Manning called him to say she had found some papers concerning the Lamberti stuffed among a stack of lottery tickets in LaPorte's office.

"I drove over there, and by the time I got there Mrs. Manning was getting nosy," said Jason sneeringly. "She said she didn't understand the papers, because there were two certificates." There was the original paper, signed by his uncle, giving the Lamberti to the orchestra.

But there was another certificate, recently made out, which was incomplete. The name of the new owner was not listed.

"I told her just to complete it, making it out to me, since I was the rightful owner," said Jason.

Mrs. Manning filled out the certificate for Jason and signed LaPorte's name, which she normally did, but then she got nosy again.

She suggested that maybe they ought to call the police in to make sure it was all right.

Jason was too close to victory by then, so Mrs. Manning ended up dead under the Carnegie Hall marquee. And he finally had the papers he needed. He burned the original.

Wilson asked the question before I did. "How did it happen that after LaPorte was dead you came and reclaimed the violin?"

Jason smiled smugly. "Well, see, I realized that even though I had the violin, I couldn't sell it. I couldn't even admit I had it."

So, he went on, after he shot LaPorte, he put the Lamberti back on the shelf!

"Then I could claim it legally, and LaPorte wasn't around to open his big yap."

Well, Wilson got Jason to go over it all and sign the statement, and then Jason muttered that everything would have been all right if we hadn't dug up his uncle's body.

"We didn't," said Wilson with a grin. "And now we won't have to."

Jason's face went into red splotches and he tried to grab the statement back.

"This is entrapment," he screamed. "I recant that statement! I want a lawyer."

I left Wilson and Nickerson to take care of that, and a week later Ariel and I drove north up through Lake George and Burlington past the granite boulders to Allen, Vermont.

We moved into a studio apartment in what had once been part of a red barn in Allen, and I became a gentleman journalist, covering town meetings and even a flower show.

In a big bed with Ariel, the world was lovely. We talked of getting married in the spring.

I wrote a story about the purchase of a new fire truck for Allen, Vermont, which was front-page news. The fire truck's siren was about the only loud noise you ever heard, and that only once in a while.

I put paper into my typewriter and started to write about New York. I wrote about the madness of it, the disgusting, endless struggle that never let you alone. Out of my typewriter came, "But then the essence of life is struggle. When you stop struggling, you die."

I had once considered that a newspaper job has a way of coming between you and everything else. I had meant a New York newspaper job, but now I realized it can happen in Vermont too.

Ariel sat at the wooden table in the studio and stared at me.

"Happy?" she asked.

"Sure," I said. "You?"

She smiled softly. "It's what I always wanted, Fitz. I feel you have to go after what you want, don't you?"

"Sure."

Then Ariel was crying. She kept it up for days, and when I asked her what was wrong she only shook her head. But we both knew.

One of the few times the clunker Monte Carlo started right up was the day I headed back down out of Vermont. It hummed to eager life and carried me zippingly along down the New York Thruway. You'd think the damned old wreck was a carrier pigeon heading instinctively for home, even if home was potholed streets.

But the trip took a lot out of the blue bomb. Like the first long-distance runner, who ran from Marathon to Athens to announce victory over the Persians and then collapsed and died, the gasper slowed as it hit the metal grid crossing the George Washington Bridge. It coasted to a halt on the ramp leading to the Henry Hudson Parkway and then clunked its last.

I arrived at the *Daily Press* the next morning on the rattling, swaying, graffiti-covered Lexington Avenue subway and walked in to face Ironhead.

He gave me a look. "Humph," he said.

Bike O'Malley greeted me with a quizzical glance. He had been unfired and was struggling out of Ironhead's doghouse.

Me too.

Bike was only too happy to hand back the few final bits of the Stradivarius story to me. Jason Lambert had changed places on Rikers Island with Mitch Rogers and was still furiously claiming entrapment. Wilson finally did have to dig up his uncle, and the District Attorney's office was preparing for what should be a pretty good trial.

There were a few letters back and forth from Vermont. Ariel wrote that she was happy as a clam and was sure I was too. I'm not so sure.

In November, Mitch Rogers and Ingrid called and insisted on giving me two tickets to Carnegie Hall to hear Dennis Hanley and Veronica Cerutti and the Metropolitan Youth Symphony Orchestra play Dvorak's symphony *From the New World*.

And that's when I found out that the youth orchestra, with Florence Hammerstein's help, had succeeded in claiming the Lamberti after all. Veronica still had the bow—but she let Dennis Hanley use it along with the Lamberti for the concert.

My date for the concert was Florence Hammerstein, who squeezed my hand and wept as she listened to Dennis play.

"Jamison would have been so proud," she told me.

"SOMETIMES HE'S JUST OUTRAGEOUS. MOST OF THE TIME, HE'S OUTRAGEOUSLY FUNNY!" –*PEOPLE*

KINKY FRIEDMAN

In these wild, witty tales of murder and mystery, he's "a hip hybrid of Groucho Marx and Sam Spade!" (*Chicago Tribune*)

____ **GREENWICH KILLING TIME**
0-425-10497-4/$3.50
A quirky crime and strange suspects take Kinky on a hard-boiled journey to the heart of New York's Greenwich Village!

____ **A CASE OF LONE STAR**
0-425-11185-7/$3.50
Country-boy Kinky goes center stage to catch a killer, at Manhattan's famous Lone Star Cafe! "A hilarious winner!"—UP

____ **WHEN THE CAT'S AWAY**
0-425-11830-4/$3.95
A purloined feline from Madison Square Garden's cat show is the tip-off to a trail of murders, drug rings, and gang wars that only Kinky could follow. "Gleams with wit and insight."—Robert B. Parker

---

Check book(s). Fill out coupon. Send to:

BERKLEY PUBLISHING GROUP
390 Murray Hill Pkwy., Dept. B
East Rutherford, NJ 07073

NAME_____
ADDRESS_____
CITY_____
STATE_____ ZIP_____

PLEASE ALLOW 6 WEEKS FOR DELIVERY.
PRICES ARE SUBJECT TO CHANGE WITHOUT NOTICE.

POSTAGE AND HANDLING:
$1.00 for one book, .25 for each additional. Do not exceed $3.50.

BOOK TOTAL $_____
POSTAGE & HANDLING $_____
APPLICABLE SALES TAX $_____
(CA, NJ, NY, PA)
TOTAL AMOUNT DUE $_____

PAYABLE IN US FUNDS.
(No cash orders accepted.)

197a

LAWRENCE SANDERS

___ THE TIMOTHY FILES	0-425-10924-0/$4.95
___ CAPER	0-425-10477-X/$4.95
___ THE EIGHTH COMMANDMENT	0-425-10005-7/$4.95
___ THE DREAM LOVER	0-425-09473-1/$4.50
___ THE PASSION OF MOLLY T.	0-425-10139-8/$4.95
___ THE FIRST DEADLY SIN	0-425-10427-3/$5.50
___ THE MARLOW CHRONICLES	0-425-09963-6/$4.50
___ THE PLEASURES OF HELEN	0-425-10168-1/$4.50
___ THE SECOND DEADLY SIN	0-425-10428-1/$4.95
___ THE SIXTH COMMANDMENT	0-425-10430-3/$4.95
___ THE TANGENT OBJECTIVE	0-425-10331-5/$4.95
___ THE TANGENT FACTOR	0-425-10062-6/$4.95
___ THE TENTH COMMANDMENT	0-425-10431-1/$4.95
___ THE TOMORROW FILE	0-425-08179-6/$4.95
___ THE THIRD DEADLY SIN	0-425-10429-X/$4.95
___ THE ANDERSON TAPES	0-425-10364-1/$4.95
___ THE CASE OF LUCY BENDING	0-425-10086-3/$4.95
___ THE SEDUCTION OF PETER S.	0-425-09314-X/$4.95
___ THE LOVES OF HARRY DANCER	0-425-08473-6/$4.95
___ THE FOURTH DEADLY SIN	0-425-09078-7/$4.95
___ TIMOTHY'S GAME	0-425-11641-7/$5.50
___ LOVE SONGS	0-425-11273-X/$4.50
___ STOLEN BLESSINGS	0-425-11872-X/$4.95
___ CAPITAL CRIMES	0-425-12164-X/$5.95

<u>Check book(s). Fill out coupon. Send to:</u>

BERKLEY PUBLISHING GROUP
390 Murray Hill Pkwy., Dept. B
East Rutherford, NJ 07073

NAME_____

ADDRESS_____

CITY_____

STATE_____ ZIP_____

PLEASE ALLOW 6 WEEKS FOR DELIVERY.
PRICES ARE SUBJECT TO CHANGE
WITHOUT NOTICE.

POSTAGE AND HANDLING:
$1.00 for one book, 25¢ for each additional. Do not exceed $3.50.

BOOK TOTAL	$____
POSTAGE & HANDLING	$____
APPLICABLE SALES TAX (CA, NJ, NY, PA)	$____
TOTAL AMOUNT DUE	$____

PAYABLE IN US FUNDS.
(No cash orders accepted.)

245a

WHITLEY STRIEBER
Author of the 7-month *New York Times* bestseller COMMUNION

MAJESTIC
THE COAST-TO-COAST BESTSELLING NOVEL!

"THRILLING!" — *Chicago Tribune*

"ENTERTAINING!" — New York *Daily News*

"INTRIGUING!" — *Washington Post*

The government lied....

A young newspaperman is handed the story of the century by the retired first director of the CIA's Operation Majestic: Something did land one night in 1947 in the New Mexico desert....

____ MAJESTIC by Whitley Strieber (on sale Oct. '90)
0-425-12295-6/$4.95

For Visa and MasterCard orders (minimum $25) call: **1-800-631-8571**

FOR MAIL ORDERS: CHECK BOOK(S). FILL OUT COUPON. SEND TO:	POSTAGE AND HANDLING: $1.00 for one book, 25¢ for each additional. Do not exceed $3.50.
BERKLEY PUBLISHING GROUP 390 Murray Hill Pkwy., Dept. B East Rutherford, NJ 07073	**BOOK TOTAL** $ ____
NAME_____	**POSTAGE & HANDLING** $ ____
ADDRESS_____	**APPLICABLE SALES TAX** $ ____ (CA, NJ, NY, PA)
CITY_____	**TOTAL AMOUNT DUE** $ ____
STATE_____ ZIP_____	**PAYABLE IN US FUNDS.** (No cash orders accepted.)
PLEASE ALLOW 6 WEEKS FOR DELIVERY. PRICES ARE SUBJECT TO CHANGE WITHOUT NOTICE.	

> "SANDFORD GRABS YOU BY THE THROAT AND WON'T LET GO...TOUGH, GRITTY, GENUINELY SCARY."
> —ROBERT B. PARKER

RULES OF PREY

John Sandford

THE TERRIFYING THRILLER!

The killer is mad but brilliant. He kills victims for the sheer contest of it and leaves notes with each body: rules of murder. Never have a motive. Never kill anyone you know...Lucas Davenport is the cop who's out to get him. And this cop plays by his own set of rules.

> "SLEEK AND NASTY...IT'S A BIG, SCARY, SUSPENSEFUL READ, AND I LOVED EVERY MINUTE OF IT!"
> —STEPHEN KING

___RULES OF PREY   0-425-12163-1/ $4.95

For Visa and MasterCard orders (minimum $25) call: 1-800-631-8571

FOR MAIL ORDERS: CHECK BOOK(S). FILL OUT COUPON. SEND TO:

BERKLEY PUBLISHING GROUP
390 Murray Hill Pkwy., Dept. B
East Rutherford, NJ 07073

NAME_____

ADDRESS_____

CITY_____

STATE_____ ZIP_____

PLEASE ALLOW 6 WEEKS FOR DELIVERY.
PRICES ARE SUBJECT TO CHANGE WITHOUT NOTICE.

POSTAGE AND HANDLING:
$1.00 for one book, 25¢ for each additional. Do not exceed $3.50.

BOOK TOTAL	$____
POSTAGE & HANDLING	$____
APPLICABLE SALES TAX (CA, NJ, NY, PA)	$____
TOTAL AMOUNT DUE	$____

PAYABLE IN US FUNDS.
(No cash orders accepted.)